WARRIOR ELF

THE WORLD OF ELVES
BOOK 3

TERRY SPEAR

PUBLISHED BY:

Terry Spear
Warrior Elf
Copyright © 2022 by Terry Spear
Cover Copyright by Frost Alexis Arts
Discover more about Terry Spear at:

http://www.terryspear.com/

Print ISBN: 978-1-63311-089-2

Ebook ISBN: 978-1-63311-088-5

SYNOPSIS

Rina is a warrior elf from a long class of shadow warrior elves on the planet Xibos, a world populated by elves, griffons, dragons, giants, pixies, fairies, trolls, merfolk, centaurs, and other fantastical creatures. They've recently had visitors from a whole other planetary system who call Xibos a primitive elf world. But Rina doesn't believe they are a primitive people in the least as she fights for right and though she earns much gold from her work, she also takes on cases where there is no hope of reward—just because it's something she must do. Fighting is in her blood. And she has a magic trick up her leather sleeve. She is all about work and no play, so when she takes on the mission of rescuing a princess from a tower—if she even really needs rescuing—Rina ends up meeting a champion elf knight—who also rights wrongs. But he works for the king of Castle Grande of the Wild Meadowlands elves and she's not sure they have the princess's best interests at heart.

Artur serves as the king's champion from a long class of champions of the Wild Meadowlands elves when he encounters a warrior elf fighting dark arts knights all on her own. He watches in fascination, until he eliminates the last one, and he's not sure what to think of her. Does she have the princess's welfare in mind? Or some darker purpose? He admires Rina, but he doesn't trust her. Yet it appears they have a common enemy and until that's resolved, he'll watch her back and hope she watches his!

To my good friend Louise Evans. We had such a lovely time visiting in Waco for lunches and book talks. Thanks for loving my books and meeting with me to have even more fun!

1

Preparing for a journey to take on a new night mission, Rina was a warrior shadow elf from a long line of warrior elves and a special class of high elves with different magical abilities on the planet Xibos, populated by elves, griffons, dragons, giants, pixies, fairies, trolls, merfolk, centaurs, and other fantastical creatures. But this mission had only to do with a Black Hills elf in crisis, she thought.

Rina's sister, Sylph, her brother, Aegis, her mother and father, her uncles, her aunts, her grandparents on both sides of the family were all warriors. Suffice it to say she was born into the role, and she was certain she would die fighting in that capacity someday. Her kind would fight for years, but when it was all said and done, they often didn't have long-life expectancies. They lived for the day, for the glory, for righting wrongs and saving those who could not save themselves.

Not to mention she wanted to leave the shadow elf lands for a while after she learned her boyfriend had cheated on her with a blue elf. A blue elf, of all things! They were their sworn enemy! He was just lucky she felt he wasn't worth killing or she would have eliminated him on the spot. Even his close friends had told him he was an idiot for risking such folly.

Rina and her siblings were cousins of the famous Dracolin Rossover, who was the Warrior Chief, son of the shadow elf's king's advisor and their age too. He was from a long line of Warrior Chiefs and had recently married Persephonice, an amazing creature that some called a landbound mermaid who could speak with all kinds of different creatures that no one else could. She called herself a langolar and no one in any of the elves' realms had heard of her kind before. She said they had come by spaceship from the sky, from another world even. Then another woman like Persephonice had come into their realm— Eloria, who ended up with Viator, crown prince of the Darkland Forest elves. Eloria was just as amazing as Persephonice, able to talk to a dragon, Talom, who would not be tamed, and befriended him. But she was also part high elf who had magical abilities. So she hadn't been a complete outsider.

Rina had wondered if any remarkable males would come from the world where Eloria and Persephonice were from, not that she had any designs on one if he did. But the idea of meeting one *was* intriguing.

Today, she was on a mission on her own, like she often was. She'd heard tales about a girl locked in the tower of a castle in the territory of the Black Hills elves. A princess, if the tale was true. Rina fathomed that did not sound like a place a princess should be, locked in a tower against her will. Rina wasn't even being paid for the mission. She didn't usually undertake an assignment like that because of the danger she put herself in. But this case intrigued her. She didn't bother to tell her family. Her sister and brother were off on jobs of their own. Her mother and father, the same. It was a wee bit out of the shadow elf territory, but she just needed to get away and see for herself if a princess needed rescuing.

Rina swept her black hair off her shoulders, one of her eyes a pretty green, the other a dazzling blue. Some would say having different eye colors made her special, others that she was cursed. Truth be told, she enjoyed her unusual eye colors and was often amused when someone would see her for the first time and be taken aback, look again, as if the person had been mistaken about what they'd seen.

She mounted her horse, Midnight, her trusty sword in its scabbard, her saddlebags packed. She was said to have been born with a sword in her hand, at least that's how the story was told for any of her warrior kind. Some battle on the horizon always needed to be fought. There was always someone who needed help in dealing with some blackguard. She loved her job and couldn't imagine doing anything else.

For two days she had traveled, riding her black stallion through the woods, valleys, and through a mountain pass. She finally reached the edge of the thick pines and oaks of Larimar Forest and said to her horse in a whisper against his velvet ear, "If you hear me whistle once, come for me. If you hear me whistle twice, run home at once." If Midnight ran home, her family, if any of them were there, would know she was in trouble and her horse would show them the way. She wouldn't call on him in the middle of danger to join her though, unless she was certain she needed a fast getaway and believed he wouldn't be injured. She certainly didn't want to risk her horse's safety for anything. He was too precious to her, her companion in battle and beyond. Which made her high elf genes different from the ones living in the mountains—also magic users, because they tamed dragons as their companions.

She slipped off the back of her horse, then crept through the woods to reach a small castle. She'd seen the golden eyes of gray wolves peering at her through the darkness, a darkness she could see in just as well as them. A large, horned owl hooted high above in a pine tree, warning there was a new danger on the prowl. Her, of course. Not a danger to the owls in the woods, but to the elves who would keep a princess locked in a tower.

She saw a couple of bearded guards outside of the castle, talking to one another about the long, cold nights and how they wished they were anywhere but here. She moved closer to more clearly hear their words.

"The king will be changing my post at the end of the week. What about you?" the blond man asked the other. They were both big men, heavily muscled. Protecting the princess? Or keeping her from leaving the tower?

"A month. I fear it will be the longest time I've ever had to serve at an isolated, disagreeable post."

"Well, just don't become cozy with the princess. The king killed the last two guards who allowed her to escape. She didn't make it beyond the ground floor, yet that was enough to send the king into a rage. He wants her married off to someone who will promise him an alliance."

Then the men grew quiet, watching their surroundings like they should have been doing all along. Rina skirted around through the woods, looking for any other guards, but saw none. The others had to be inside. The stone fortifications were thirty feet tall, the walls at least fifteen feet thick, substantial enough to prevent unwanted visitors from entering the keep, but not her.

Not only did Rina have her trusty sword, her magic, and her stealth, she could climb walls like a chameleon, blending in, slithering upward, and no one would be the wiser. She had to reach the tower window and see for herself if the princess was indeed a prisoner there.

Marrying off royal sons and daughters to forge alliances was often done, so it wasn't a given that the girl was in any real danger, except from herself if she should pursue attempting to escape her captors. Rina couldn't imagine a princess being able to live in the wilderness on her own. Not like a warrior elf could live off the land, fight evil, and survive the challenging weather —lightning storms, snowstorms, windstorms, you name it.

Rina had already breached the wall and saw a couple of guards peering out at the woods from the wall walk to the north of her, oblivious to her climbing down to make her way to the tower.

The place was deserted except for a stable hand exercising a horse in the inner baily. She just needed to reach the side of the tower without being seen and make her climb. Vines would help to give her something to hold onto and offer her a modicum of cover, but her ability to blend in with the red stones would ensure she was unseen as she made her way up the tall tower. She saw no one within range that could spy her, no windows that looked out this way except for the one tower window about forty feet high, and no guards on the wall walk on this side either—they were all on the other side where they suspected their greatest threat would come. She was free to race across the open space between the wall walk to the tower, throw herself at the wall, and begin the climb.

She was known for her speed and agility, often beating her sister out, not her brother though, and was halfway up the tower wall when she heard someone say to the guards down below, "King Leogane will be here in short order. Be alert. We don't want him to think we're not sufficiently guarding the princess."

The voice was that of a middle-aged woman, gruff and stern. She must be in charge of watching out for the princess, Rina thought. She continued to climb up the wall, grasping narrow finger holds, using the toes of her pointed boots to poke between the brickwork to continue making her way up the tall tower wall as the woman returned to the keep and the men grumbled to themselves about having way too many bosses. That's what Rina loved about her job. She would usually have one boss only per assignment. Except when she was on a mission of her own where she wasn't receiving any payment. Payment was always welcome, but no bosses was also nice.

Rina was nearly to the window when she heard a woman pacing inside. She knew it was a woman due to her light footsteps crossing the wooden floor. Then Rina peered inside the window and saw a room that was austere, not as lavish as she thought a princess's chamber should be. Simple bed linens, a small bed, a table and two chairs, very sparsely furnished. No tapestries on the walls to keep out the chill, no carpet on the floor either. The girl was alone, and Rina wondered if she could gain the girl's confidence without frightening her to death. The blond-haired girl looked to be about Rina's age, twenty or so, but Rina was sure the princess would have been coddled all her life and wouldn't know how to fight. Rina thought to take her home with her and after that, decide what to do with her, soliciting her family's advice. At least her parents were good about letting her and her siblings handle a situation they felt needed resolution without telling them outright what to do.

In that regard, Rina and her siblings made their own mistakes, owned them, and had to deal with the repercussions. Which meant in this case, dealing with the princess's father, who most likely would want Rina's head. But she had to learn the truth. Was the princess in any real danger?

She wondered who King Leogane was. A suitor? Wouldn't he object to the princess being confined like she was? Or maybe that was the only way the king could keep the princess from running away from her obligations. If the king was an ogre, and Rina's parents agreed, she would attempt to steal the princess away to some other realm and let another kingdom take care of her.

Rina had to take into account that the princess might be confined for her own good. That she was wayward and needed someone to control her willfulness. What did Rina know? She worked too hard to be rebellious and not do what needed to be done.

Looking highly agitated, the girl was pacing, wearing a black gown sweeping the floor, her skin washed out, probably from not getting outside enough to soak up the sun, her shoes merely slippers to be worn inside. She needed boots to run in, though Rina had an extra pair that would probably fit the girl. Rina hoped she was wrong, and that the princess was fine and that this was her lot in life, but if it wasn't...Rina had every intention of rescuing her.

2

Artur was an elf from a long line of knightly champions who had served King Leogane and his ancestors forever. To Artur's deep regret, his older brother before him had served well and had died in combat during a battle with a neighboring force. Now Artur was the king's companion and loyal friend and guard as they made their way to the stronghold in the Black Hills. He oft spoke to the king about matters that others wouldn't dare speak to him about—like who he should wed and who he should stay well away from. Despite being a warrior, Artur believed in romance, love, and chivalry and because Leogane was interested in wedding his advisor's daughter, he felt the king should marry her. Forget going for the spoiled princess locked in the tower just because the king could make an alliance with another, whom Artur didn't trust in the least.

Artur could imagine all kinds of difficulties with this princess. Who wouldn't want to wed the king? But her uncle had warned how unruly she could be, and the king would have to use a firm hand on her.

But Leogane was good of heart, good to his people, wanting

only to keep them safe, working, fed, and happy. From every-thing Artur could learn about the princess, she would try any man's patience. She should support the king as his queen, stand by him, feel the same way about his people as the king did because they would be her people also if he wed her, but he doubted she would do any of that.

At least Leogane was seriously considering Artur's words and said he only wanted to meet her and see for himself if she was truly the ogre some said she was.

Leogane was riding beside his chief advisor, Erlig, then glanced back to see Artur riding behind him. "Come ride with me."

"Aye." Artur quickly rode up beside the king and the king's advisor dropped back with a nod to Artur, the trail too narrow for more than two to ride abreast in here.

"You look so glum. Even my advisor doesn't seem as worried as you about my marrying the princess when it would be Erlig's daughter I would wed instead." Leogane smiled at Artur.

"'Tis because Erlig doesn't believe you will actually wish to take the woman for your wife, I suspect. Sometimes a woman can deceive a man into changing his mind."

Leogane chuckled. "You speak from experience, aye?"

Artur may believe in love and protecting the one he loved, but no, he had never experienced a courtly love and Leogane knew it. "I've seen it oft enough." Which was true. Some of his warrior friends had even become smitten with a woman who would turn on her heel and leave them destitute while the woman dallied with other men. He'd worried about his friend, Dracolin, the shadow elf Warrior Chief, when he had found a mermaid who walked on legs, so they said, and fallen hard for her, despite everyone warning him not to. Artur had met her and other than her beautiful fall of red hair and her pretty green eyes, she didn't look like a mermaid to him in the least. But she could swim. Something most elves could not do. The blue elves, the ones who lived by the waterways or the oceans and lakes, they swam. But they were rather the exception.

"Do not fear. I am not making any decision about the woman any time soon," Leogane said.

Good. But women could change the stoutest men's minds when they were least expecting it, so Artur was wary about the king even meeting her.

Then the birds in the forest took off in a frantic flight heavenward warning of imminent danger. Artur shouted to their knightly escort, "Prepare for battle!"

He and the king and the rest of his men readied their swords. Artur could kill the beasts that were plaguing them on this journey just as easily with his crossbow and bolts, having been trained by the masters of the bow also. But for now, he watched, listened, breathed deeply of the air, anticipating another onslaught of the knights that had fought them along this trail twice already. Artur suspected it all had to do with Leogane's meeting with the princess.

PRINCESS MIRABELLA STOPPED PACING and glanced at the window, not sure what had made her look. Nothing ever happened at the window, yet she had a strong feeling that she needed to turn and check it out. Startling her, she saw a female elf dressed as a warrior in black leather, spiky metal points on her bracers to fight against an enemy in hand-to-hand-combat, peering in at her. Mirabella gasped. She wasn't afraid of her, just shocked to see the girl peering through the tower window that was forty feet above the ground.

The black-haired girl smiled at her, her unique blue and

green eyes and warm smile captivating Mirabella in an instant. She recognized her aura that identified her as a shadow elf.

There were no bars to keep Mirabella from escaping. The drop would kill her, so how did the girl get there? Mirabella should have cried out, should have screamed with fright. She did neither and studied the pretty girl, her long silky, black hair such a contrast to Mirabella's light blond hair.

"Who are you?" Mirabella whispered to the girl who couldn't have been much older than her. Mirabella needn't have kept her voice hushed since no one could hear her through the tower walls. The blocks of rock mortared together were eight feet thick.

"I am Rina, a shadow elf warrior, your rescuer, should you need rescuing."

Mirabella's mouth gaped. Her prayers had been answered! She'd prayed she could find someone to rescue her from the tower but now only one single female warrior elf was here to save her? Or maybe more were in the woods waiting and this one was sent to tell her they were here to aid her. Mirabella knew they couldn't fight the guards inside the tower and the ones outside to make her escape without a lot of help.

"Do you need rescuing?" Rina asked. Her manner was calm, collected, when Mirabella felt anything but.

Mirabella frowned at her. What if they should find the warrior elf trying to save her? They would kill Rina! "Aye, I do need rescuing. I've been imprisoned here by my uncle."

"Because?"

Mirabella hated telling the story to anyone, making her relive the horror, but also because no one believed her. "I witnessed him murdering my father, the true king, on a hunt. No one who was involved in the hunting 'accident' that day knew I had seen what had happened. My nanny wouldn't let me join my father on the hunt. I snuck out anyway." She tilted her chin up, not about to shed any more tears over it. "I want to avenge my father's death, and take over the rule of my people, but he intends to marry me off to make an alliance and my husband will not believe me either. What if he were to lock me away in a tower next? I have to do what is right by my father and I will do anything to make that happen."

Rina smiled, and Mirabella thought she didn't believe her. Nobody did, so there was nothing surprising in that. Still, if the warrior elf was here to rescue her, then Mirabella would do everything in her power to convince her that she needed rescuing.

"May I know your name?"

Rina didn't know who Mirabella was? She wasn't sure she should even trust the warrior now. "I'm Princess Mirabella, a Black Hills elf. I will reward you in any way I can, once I'm freed from the tower and can regain what is by rights mine," Mirabella quickly said.

"Saving you is enough of a reward," Rina said.

Mirabella couldn't believe it. But she would reward the woman anyway, if she was able to oust her uncle from his rule over her people. "What must I do?" Mirabella couldn't believe she would have the chance to leave the tower like this, but how was Rina supposed to accomplish this? She truly must have a group of warriors with her beyond the castle walls and they were only awaiting word from her to rescue Mirabella.

Then they heard the sound of footfalls approaching her tower chamber and Mirabella quickly looked at the door. "Can you hold on?" she whispered to Rina.

Rina nodded.

Mirabella would have to leave with Rina *after* the woman who was watching over her left her alone again. Mirabella hoped Rina could hold onto the tower wall long enough without falling. She glanced back at the window, but Rina had already disappeared.

Mirabella heard the key in the lock in the door, but she couldn't help herself. She rushed to the window and looked out, fearing Rina had fallen but there was no sign of her. Mirabella frowned. She couldn't imagine what had become of Rina. Had she flown away? She didn't have wings, or at least that Mirabella had seen. Was she a magic user with some kind of an ability Mirabella hadn't heard of? She hadn't a clue. She hoped it would mean that Rina could secret her away in the same manner in which she'd secreted herself away.

She leaned out the window of the fourth floor of the circular tower at Mayden Castle, wishing she could fly away like the eagles and hawks that soared high above Larimar Forest, not something that a Black Hill's elf was capable of. She wished she could steal a horse and ride unnoticed through the Grandmere Pass to the shadow elf kingdom. That she could slip away into the dense forests, beyond the Black Hills, and disappear forever from the home that was no longer hers until she could oust the usurper who was her uncle. What lay beyond the Five Sisters of Kintail, the mountains that dominated the northern sky? What lay west beyond Larimar Forest? And east? She'd heard savages lived there by the sea, bloodthirsty pirates who raped and pillaged, took everything they could carry away, then burned villagers' homes to the ground. If her uncle was supposed to be so powerful, why did he not lock these brigands in the dungeon or eliminate them with his powerful army? Her army, if she could regain control.

Instead, she was the one held hostage, as if she could be any real threat to anyone. Yet, she could. If she reclaimed the throne. She looked south, and though she could not see the castle there, she knew it was where her mother had taken her last breath, giving birth to Mirabella. It was where Uncle Inari had turned on her father and murdered him in cold blood to gain his throne. Moreover, it was there that King Inari ruled with an iron fist, commanding all to bow to his whim.

But *her*. He could never rule *her*.

As the gods were her witnesses, she again vowed she would free her people from her uncle's tyrannical rule.

Mighty plans, she chastised herself when she still hadn't managed to free herself from the tower and castle grounds, though the gods knew she'd tried. She'd never been allowed to leave the perfectly smooth, conical stone structure once she'd grown old enough to successfully attempt escape. No one had taught her how to cook, or sew, or heal the sick. She knew nothing about the outside world because of her sheltered life. With the wild animals roaming freely about the forests, and not even a way to start a fire, nor any knowledge of which plants were edible...

Shaking her head, she knew she'd be dead within a week, if not sooner.

She clenched her fists, stifling the despair that wrenched at her courage, threatening to destroy her resolve at making another escape attempt. A time of celebration—her twentieth birthday only three days away, meant only that her prison sentence here would end, and begin anew with her marriage to King Leogane, her uncle's ally in all battles, big or small, at some other castle, she knew not where.

None of the guards or servants she managed to speak to knew anything about Leogane except that he was a warrior who excelled at battle, and that his name meant lion, which didn't bode well. If any knew anything more than that, they would not say.

ARTUR SHEATHED HIS SWORD, checking on all their men, making sure no one was injured and reported back to the king. "We are all in good stead. I believe whoever has sent these knights to attack us is only doing so to prevent you from reaching the princess." Though Artur still had reservations about her, he didn't like it when someone tried to keep him from his mission. He knew the king felt likewise.

"I believe the same as you," the king said, his advisor nodding. "Which makes me all the more determined to see her."

"Unless they have disguised themselves as Vladek's men, I believe he is trying to thwart you."

"Aye. He will not do so. Let's continue on our trek. The sooner we arrive, the sooner we can finish this," the king said, and they continued on their way.

Artur just hoped they could successfully reach the keep, learn that Leogane wasn't interested in the princess, and when they left, they would no longer be plagued with attacks.

At least for now, they had been successful at repelling the attacks, but what if the enemy's numbers increased even more?

3

Rina knew stealing the princess away from the tower would be a job and a half, but she was always up for the most challenging of assignments. The good thing was that this was a mission worthy of taking on and she hadn't climbed the tower for naught. A princess in distress, her father murdered, her usurper of an uncle seated on the throne? A perfect mission. It didn't matter that Rina wouldn't earn anything for the job. The princess had nothing to give her. All Rina could hope for was to free her from this place and take her somewhere to keep her safe.

She needed to ask the princess more questions though. About the timing of the guards' rotations. At what times did her staff go to see her? Did Mirabella have traveling clothes that could aid her escape? Rina had extra clothes for the princess in her saddlebags just in case, but she thought it would be easier to climb the tower and see to the situation first. Then she heard someone walking to the princess's chamber door, and she needed to hide against the outer wall, away from the window, so whoever it was wouldn't sound the alarm that she was here, clinging to the wall. She could just imagine a shower of arrows headed her way.

She moved away from the window, clung to the wall, and listened to a key trying to be jammed into a lock, but the key didn't fit. Somehow, she had to come up with a foolproof plan to free the princess.

MIRABELLA HEARD the key in the lock in the door, but she leaned further out the window, searching to see if Rina had climbed higher instead of down to the ground, but she saw no sign of her up above either.

Another key was inserted in the lock to her door, and she wondered why the woman just didn't keep the key to the room separate from all the rest so she wouldn't have to try all the keys out every time. Several keys had grated in the lock of her door, and finally one made the clicking sound that meant the key holder had finally found the right one. Mirabella jumped off the seat and wheeled around, her heart thundering. She knew no one would suspect she'd make another escape attempt, not now that two stout male guards accompanied the servants when they brought her food or bathwater. Not after the last time that she managed to overpower the woman who was in charge of her, the scrawny-faced Phiri, once a lady-in-waiting to her mother, but now, just her captor. Her heart sped up with concern just the same.

The heavy oak door swung open, and Phiri walked in, a tray in her hands. Her icy blue eyes took in Mirabella's appearance as they always did, ensuring that Mirabella was still alive and well.

Mirabella straightened her gown and she put on her usual

annoyed expression because the woman always looked so annoyed at her, as if she couldn't stand working for her.

"Your face is flushed. You're not feverish, are you?" Phiri dropped the tray on the table where two chairs sat, one for Mirabella and one for her, but she didn't wait for a response, as if she really didn't care. "Eat up and be quick about it. Your betrothed comes to...inspect you."

"Leogane," Mirabella squeaked out, her skin instantly chilled. She hadn't meant to sound like a mouse, and she quickly recovered, stiffening her back and hardening her eyes. "Why would he need to *inspect* me?" She walked over to the table for two and lifted a piece of bread from the tray. She still had high hopes that Rina and her party of warriors would rescue her before that happened.

She'd even stopped eating for a time, but that hadn't worked. Her uncle had merely beaten a serving girl in front of her, and she quickly learned starving herself wasn't the solution.

Phiri's thin lips curved upward, but no warmth reached her eyes. "He doesn't want *you*; seems there's someone else he prefers to wed. Imagine that? Not want the daughter of the former king of Black Hills and now the niece of his brother, the king?" The woman swiped a blueberry tart from the tray and lifted it to her lips with her little finger elevated as if she were seated at a royal dinner.

There was no need for pretense here.

Mirabella dropped onto a wooden chair and poked a spoon into a boar-and-brasey broth. "What does my uncle say about this?"

"Since Leogane doesn't want you, King Inari has asked him to see you here in case you can change his mind. That's what. But I doubt you will be suitable to him." Phiri motioned to a girl about Mirabella's age, standing near the doorway. "Justina, bring Princess Mirabella's new gown, and be quick about it."

Mirabella didn't recognize the girl, but then that wasn't so unusual. Her uncle often switched out the staff to ensure that none of them grew fond of her. Phiri was the exception. She hated Mirabella for killing her mother in childbirth. The woman had told her that often enough. It meant she had lost her position as the queen's maid and confidant and living in the beautiful castle where Mirabella had been born, though she didn't remember what it looked like all that well any longer. Just the gardens that her mother had adored, according to Phiri, and Mirabella wanted to see them.

At first, Mirabella had cried about her lot in life, but the tears had dried up long ago. She'd hardened herself, the only way she could deal with this. No one had cared about what happened to her, and she had to take control of her life. Apparently, Leogane disapproved of her as well. He didn't even know her!

The guards and servants were careful not to get close to her, fearing reprisals from the king. They had reason to fear him. Mirabella had accomplished thirty-three escapes over the years, though she hadn't managed to get very far. Many of the staff, if not all, were wary of her.

Then hope flickered. Mirabella almost allowed herself a smile but quashed the notion when she saw Phiri watching her. Surely, Leogane would give her some freedom if Rina was unable to get her out of here beforehand. If so, she would escape him on the trail. It could make it much easier for Rina to help her then. Mirabella would not be the wife to any who pledged his allegiance to Inari. Destroying Inari was the only notion that had kept her sane for the last eleven years.

"What are you thinking, princess?" Phiri asked, her eyes narrowed. "You have a way of looking past a body when you are planning something. Your jaw tightens and..." She glanced down at Mirabella's hands. "You clench your fists."

Mirabella unclenched her hands, made an effort to relax her

expression, and grabbed her spoon again. The boar, onions, and potatoes that swam in the thick creamy broth tasted especially good this afternoon. She wondered if Phiri sampled a good enough quantity before every meal, though as thin as she was, she looked like she ate nothing more than a pigeon's egg daily. "I was thinking how much I would not like to see this man, who does not wish me for a bride."

"Tsk, tsk, my lady. 'Tis not your choice, but his. Moreover, if you have any idea of making him dislike you anymore than he already does, think again. King Inari has another nobleman in mind for you, and I am certain he would be even more to your dislike. Though rumors abound he wishes your hand and is angered the king has chosen Leogane over him. Nevertheless, Leogane has been loyal to Inari for some years, whereas, Count Vladek has only just begun to take an interest in the Black Hills. He lives beyond the Five Sisters of Kintail and nothing is known about his people, but it is rumored your mother came from there."

"My mother?" Mirabella asked, her voice shaky. She nearly dropped her spoon in the bowl. Why hadn't she ever considered her mother might not have been from this kingdom? Did her mother have sisters or brothers? A father or mother still alive? Surely, one of them would take her in. Maybe they could help her to take back her kingdom, with power and positions and wealth to pay for their aid.

Phiri acted as though Mirabella had said nothing. She rattled on. "Still, if Leogane doesn't wish you, the king intends to offer you to Vladek. He has already said he wants you, sight unseen." She raised a dark brow. "Though I think the king is a bit suspicious of why this Vladek suddenly is interested in King Inari's niece. But the notion of tying another region under his jurisdiction that he has no control over now appeals." Phiri snatched the last of the blueberry tarts. "Quit dawdling with your food."

The girl with Mirabella's new gown cleared her throat as she reentered the chamber.

Phiri motioned for the maid to bring her the dark green velvet gown. "If you are eating no more than that, it is time to dress, *princess*."

She was the only one Mirabella knew who could make the title of princess sound like a disease. Mirabella stared at the fabric with annoyance. "You know I only wear black."

"You have been in mourning for your father for eleven years. 'Tis long enough. And the black does nothing for your pale complexion."

A bell clanged in the inner courtyard and Mirabella's heart jumped. It only sounded when the king arrived, though there had been no mention he was coming, so she assumed it was for Leogane.

"God's teeth," Phiri said, her face red. "What is he doing here so soon? Stand outside the door," she ordered the guards. "Time to change your gown, princess."

Mirabella stood, hating that her legs felt like soggy bread. She'd never feared anyone, save her uncle, a brutal man, who was used to getting his way.

Though Phiri expected Mirabella to stand up and have her gown exchanged, instead, she headed for the window, knocking over a vase holding a single blood rose in her haste, and rescued it off the floor. Then peering out of the window, she endeavored to see what the man looked like. Thirty men rode into the inner bailey, stirring up dirt, scattering chickens that squawked and sent a flurry of feathers flying, like a sudden snowstorm.

All of the men wore armor to protect themselves from wild animals in the shire and from evil men who prayed on the weak.

All wore helmets, and all looked the same from her prison forty feet above the ground.

One looked up to see her peeking out the narrow window while she breathed in the rose's sweet fragrance. Then, as if given an order to look too, everyone shifted their gazes upward, following the first man's gaze.

Her whole body heated, though she did not duck away from the window, just glowered at them. She was certain they could not see the look of contempt on her face from this distance. When they began to dismount, their attention turned to the servants who took their horses. Phiri roughly tugged her away from the window. "Unless you wish the king to see you naked first, you best come away from there while you dress."

She scoffed under her breath and set the rose in a tankard of water, wondering why she hadn't seen any sign of the warrior elf. She prayed Rina and her companions would rescue Mirabella on the road.

Within minutes, Mirabella was wearing the forest green velvet dress and thought how easy it would be to blend in with the woods, though she was not altogether happy about wearing anything other than black. Not until her uncle hanged for murdering her father. Then she would wear any color she chose. But this would work for the woods, she thought. Then again, she really needed to wear trews and a shirt, not a long gown that would catch on the underbrush and tree branches when she made her escape.

After braiding her hair with pearls, Phiri looked her over and nodded. "That will do."

A knock ensued and when Justina answered the door, the guard said to Phiri, "His Majesty, King Leogane wishes to see Princess Mirabella at once. He has other pressing business to attend to and doesn't wish to be delayed."

"I thought he would stay the evening," Phiri said. "I thought he would sup with her tomorrow before he left. How will he decide if he wants her if he doesn't spend any time with her?" She spoke in an annoyed way, not truly asking the question of any. "Very well, princess, come, and be quick..."

"About it," Mirabella said, wondering if the woman could ever think of something different to say.

Phiri narrowed her eyes at her. She wasn't allowed to beat Mirabella, only her uncle had that privilege, but the woman gave her looks that could kill in lieu of the beatings. A time or two Mirabella was sure Phiri added something to her food that made her sicker than a worm-ridden dog.

Through the cold hall to the circular stone steps and all the way down to the bottom floor, Mirabella reminded herself that she would most likely be able to escape Leogane with Rina and her companions' assistance should he want Mirabella, though she couldn't help the way her legs shook or the way her stomach wouldn't quit flip-flopping all over the place.

Between being annoyed the king would look her over like she was a side of beef, and the fact that no male had ever paid her any mind the nearly eleven years she'd been held a prisoner, she couldn't help the way her body reacted to her fear. Luckily, the long sleeves that draped down to the hem of her skirt at the back of her wrists covered the chill bumps dotting her arms. But she was sure her face would reveal much more than she wished to. Either she'd lose all the color in her face if the man was a beast, or her cheeks would flame rose red if he looked at her in an interested way.

～

RINA HAD SNEAKED down the tower wall and finally made her way inside the castle through an open window. From there, she slipped down the corridor, staying close to the wall in case she needed to suddenly blend into it.

Every time she heard the servers' footfalls as they headed to the great hall carrying dishes of food, she held herself still against a stone wall. She wanted to sneak into the great hall and witness everything for herself. To see what this Leogane was truly like. To see if the princess might actually be happy to marry him, in which case, Rina's job would be done. Leogane would take care of the princess and deal with her murderous uncle, if everything worked out as planned.

But Rina wouldn't leave it to chance. She had to know for sure.

She finally reached the great hall and peeked in. Servers were filling tankards with wine, setting platters of food on tables. Armored knights numbering—she counted each and every one of them—thirty, including the man sitting in the very center of the high table, black haired, imperious, the king. She slipped in and made herself invisible against the wall. Sitting on either side of the king would be his most trusted, loyal, and revered companions. One of the men was older, probably his wise old advisor, his hair brown but graying. The other man was younger, more Rina's age, possibly the king's champion. Now, he caught her attention with his long blond hair and blue eyes, his gaze taking in the servers, the guards of Mayden Castle, watching everyone and everything, wary like a warrior who was ready to protect the king at all costs at any given moment. Except he'd missed seeing Rina slipping into the great hall.

She realized there really was no one of any importance staying here to welcome the king. No lords or ladies. The only one of any consequence was the princess herself who was dressing for the occasion in her bedchamber.

Then the princess made her appearance alongside the woman who taunted her with so much scorn. Rina wanted to get rid of the woman first thing! The meek maid Justina was holding back behind the two of them as the princess made her way into the great hall.

The princess held her head high as if she would not be cowed, but she looked very ill at ease. Rina wanted to join her and show her she had someone in her court to back her up, but she figured Leogane's men and Mirabella's uncle's guards would kill Rina—the intruder—on the spot.

TEN OF LEOGANE'S men sat at the elevated table, and Mirabella wondered if they were the king and his senior advisors. Servants had hastily prepared a meal for the king and his men of the same foods she had been offered. Her chin held high, she walked toward the table, bypassing the rest of the tables filled with Leogane's knights, two stout fierce-looking guards quickly taking their place at her side. All they needed were barbed collars and drooling jowls to make the picture more complete. Her uncle had removed any guard who'd seemed in the least bit sympathetic to her cause, and since then had found the nastiest, ugliest beasts to guard her.

Phiri and Justina hung back at the entrance to the great hall, waiting to hear what was said. Feeling she was going forward to her execution, Mirabella imagined the executioner moving her hair to the top of her head, readying her neck for his blade. The hair on the nape of her neck stood on end.

The man sitting at the center of the table—his shoulder-length hair black as a bottomless well, his eyes ice blue, but clearer than Phiri's, his lips set in a thin grim line—watched her approach like a hawk targeted a rabbit for its next meal. A scar cut across his cheek, leaving an angry white welt raised against bronzed skin. His dark brows narrowed at the sight of her, and she wasn't sure then if she'd be able to escape this man's cage any more than she could escape her uncle's. She had it in mind that going with Count Vladek who wanted her sight unseen, and who lived among her mother's people, might be a better choice.

"I have been told you do not wish me," she said, tilting her chin up even further.

Phiri gasped. The king said nothing, but stared at her, seemingly surprised she would speak, and probably more than surprised at the words she conveyed.

She continued, "Therefore, I offer myself to Count Vladek." Mirabella curtseyed in the courtliest manner possible, turned, and headed back to the isolation of her chamber where she would await the next of her suitors, who, hopefully, wouldn't arrive before Rina could aid in Mirabella's escape from the castle. At least that was the plan.

Though if Vladek wasn't already her uncle's ally, maybe *he* would fight him, and she would regain her father's kingdom in that way. She smiled, her stomach in turmoil, her legs shaky, but her feet already having covered a goodly distance to the exit of the great hall.

"Hold!" the king boomed.

At least she assumed it was the king the way he yelled at her, the sound reverberating off the stone walls of the large room. She paused, as if she'd turned to stone, expecting a beating like her uncle would give her. But she kept her back to Leogane, and wouldn't acknowledge him in anyway, other than not moving forward to the shelter of her chamber, like she wanted to do with all her heart.

"Bring her here!"

Mirabella suspected Leogane was furious with her for not turning to face him at the very least. It was rude to ignore her potential husband in that way. But she hoped it would seal the deal for him to give up on wanting her, if he had any notion of the kind, and she would have a chance to leave here with Rina.

At once, the guards seized her arms and turned her around, then marched her straight back to the head table. Though she tried to keep up appearances, she felt as though a sudden blizzard had encased her whole body in a block of ice and she imagined her face was just as colorless.

Leogane glowered at her, his gaze focused on her eyes, as if he were showing her who commanded her now, his face ablaze and his jaw ticking with anger.

She tried to wriggle free, but the guards only gripped her tighter.

Lifting his tankard, the king took a swig of his wine, then slammed the copper tankard down with a bang.

Did he think to intimidate her? Only her uncle did. And only because he murdered or beat those who didn't agree with him. The only thing that had spared her most of the time was she lived apart from him. She didn't believe the king would truly beat or kill her, though the angry look on his face indicated he wished to.

"You will not make my decision for me. You—"

"I understand you don't want me. Count Vladek—"

"Cease your prattle, woman!"

She was a princess! She gritted her teeth and narrowed her eyes. If he took her as his wife, she would make every effort to escape her new imprisonment.

4

In the great hall of Castle Mayden, Artur was totally amused at Princess Mirabella's behavior toward King Leogane. Artur had to maintain his stoic posture to keep from laughing out loud or invite the king's rebuke. Artur folded his arms at the head table where he was seated on one side of the king, Erlig on the other. Now would the king see the folly in taking the princess as his wife?

The rest of their men were seated at the lower tables, everyone enjoying a meal before they had to leave and travel again, the princess entertaining all of them.

Yet when Artur glanced at the king to see his outlook on this whole matter, he realized Leogane actually appeared to be intrigued! His brow was furrowed, but Artur swore his blue eyes sparkled with mirth, and even a glimmer of a smile tugged at his lips. Artur had known when Leogane saw the woman, it would be the king's undoing. She was beautiful with long, blond hair and the prettiest blue eyes. Her skin was a bit pale, but she had a kissable mouth, even when it was pinched with annoyance. She had looked them over, trying to figure out who the king was,

Artur was certain, then dismissed the king as though she had the right to do so.

She'd thrown down the gauntlet in a challenge—prove to her that the king couldn't make her bend to his whim—and Leogane couldn't resist a challenge.

Artur sighed. Which meant? They would be travelling back to their kingdom, most likely fighting the same dark knights who had besieged them, only with a prize princess in their midst that they would have to protect this time.

Artur looked beyond the king to see what Erlig thought of the matter. He wore the same controlled but amused expression. Artur figured Erlig thought the same as him about the king's interest in the princess. Maybe Leogane would change his mind once he'd gotten to know her better on their travels back to their home. A woman who could navigate the perils of the return journey in a satisfactory way could sway the king to see past her other faults. But if she couldn't even travel well or was a holy terror the whole time, then she would decide her own fate.

LEOGANE HAD AGREED with Mirabella's uncle to check out his niece to see if she was in the least bit appealing. He wouldn't take a wife who didn't interest him no matter that he would get an alliance out of it with the powerful king. He had his own army and lands and resources. Not expecting King Inari to suddenly offer his only niece to Leogane in marriage, all his own plans had been scattered to the wind. They'd had their difficulties with other forces surrounding their kingdoms, and they needed peace for both their kingdoms to prosper. He had every intention of marrying his chief advisor's daughter, the dark-haired beauty, Callie, sweet and civil-tongued, the opposite of everything Princess Mirabella seemed to be. Hot headed, ill mannered, spoiled rotten, and used to getting her way, he imagined. Even now, he could see she thought she was the one making the decisions around here. He shook his head and leaned back on the fur-covered chair.

Her golden hair was neatly braided in two long ropes extending to her knees and decorated in shimmering pearls. The soft green velvet gown swept over her slight figure, but her liquid brown eyes turned nearly black and her full pink lips scowling back at him made him believe she would make the worst sort of bride. She seemed to despise him as much as he loathed marrying her just to produce an heir and gain an ally.

He shook his head at the ludicrous thought. He had every intention of looking her over and rejecting her. That was his plan until the viper told him she'd offer herself to Count Vladek. No one knew anything of the man, except that he was uncommonly handsome, dark-haired and eyed, and had a mesmerizing quality about him. Even King Inari seemed to be drawn under Vladek's spell, when here Leogane had fostered the best of relations with the king for the most part and might lose that edge if the king gave his niece to Vladek instead.

Besides, a smoldering inferno still raged deep inside him, as he believed the attacks on him and his men, three times on their way to Castle Mayden, were more than mere coincidence. Some of Count Vladek's men? Sent to discourage him in his task?

His jaw set, Leogane deepened his voice and firmly said, "You will return with me to Castle Grande."

Her mouth dropped open and her eyes widened.

He smiled, enjoying for the moment that he'd jousted with her and won. Turning to Phiri, he said, "Have the lady dressed and ready for the long journey ahead. You may send the young girl standing beside you to accompany her."

"What about me?" Phiri asked, her voice shrill.

"What about you?" he asked, annoyed. The woman looked

like she would die on the journey she was so thin, and he wouldn't risk it. Besides, once he returned home, he would have his own women selected to take care of the princess, not someone of Inari's choice. Even the woman who accompanied her now would be sent home after they arrived safely at the castle.

Phiri straightened her shoulders and tried to make herself appear more determined or perhaps more in charge of the situation. "I have been given the mission to watch over Princess Mirabella until she has wed, by order of the king himself."

Leogane narrowed his eyes and leaned forward. "Do as I said now," he growled. He was not used to underlings telling him they wouldn't do as he commanded.

"At once, my lord." Phiri quickly curtsied, then motioned to the guards. "Hurry, bring her with us and be quick about it!"

For now, he didn't intend to wed the woman. Instead, he would observe her actions for the next couple of weeks. If she was a holy terror as he suspected, Count Vladek could have her with Leogane's blessing. If she wasn't...

Leogane didn't even want to go down that dark alley.

ONE OF THE things about Rina's jobs that she loved, she never knew how things would change and create a different opportunity to resolve them. That was the thing about it. She didn't look at it as a stumbling block, but more as a steppingstone in a new direction. She was still standing hidden in the great hall and had overheard the king tell Mirabella she would change into riding clothes and leave with him to go to his castle. It couldn't have been more perfect. He'd dismissed the woman who was in charge of Mirabella, and that was a good thing, because Rina figured she would have torn into the woman and may have created more trouble.

Rina thought she could slip in close to Mirabella and serve and protect her this way. The other girl who would be travelling with the princess looked mousy and afraid and couldn't protect a flea on one of the mangy mutts lying on the great hall's stone floor.

Somehow, Rina had to offer a story that would convince Leogane that she should be with the princess. She'd heard some of his men grumbling about the treacherous forest. About the knights who had attacked them and attempted to kill some of Leogane's knights. Rina could offer her warrior skills as the princess's bodyguard better than any male elf could because she could stay with her in her own tent. She just had to convince Leogane she was trustworthy and not intending to harm the princess or steal her away.

Truthfully, if Leogane turned out to be one of the good guys, and would offer to help Princess Mirabella regain her throne, Rina's job would be done once she helped protect her while reaching Leogane's castle. She would just have to see.

5

Within the hour, the party had departed Castle Mayden, several of Leogane's best trained knights, dressed in chain mail and ready for any battle, Princess Mirabella and her maid, Justina, the girl not much older than the princess, about her height, but dark-haired and quiet, and King Leogane, who couldn't help wondering if he'd lost his mind. He noticed Justina seemed much relieved to leave Castle Mayden behind, unlike the princess who pouted.

Leogane glanced over his shoulder to see the princess and her maid riding behind him in silence. Mirabella avoided looking at him, just watched straight ahead as men rode on either side of the ladies and others followed behind. The trail was wider here but would narrow way up ahead. Three more knights scouted up ahead, while two rode in front of Leogane, ever vigilant in watching for an ambush. He had no doubt whoever had sent men to attack them before, would do so again, but he was certain, they would be careful not to injure the princess.

Justina's gaze caught his, then she looked over at her mistress, and back to Leogane. He wondered then how long the girl had served the princess. What secrets could she tell him? Once they stopped for the night, he would question her thoroughly. In the meantime, he would question Mirabella. "Ride up with me, princess!" Leogane commanded.

She kicked her horse to a canter and joined him, refusing to look his way.

Her action both amused and annoyed him. He studied the tilt of her proud chin and of her royal bearing, wondering for the first time why she'd been locked away at the isolated Castle Mayden. Except for a small guard force, and a smaller number of servants, the naturally well-fortified castle and grounds were not used for anything else that he could see, but to house one ill-tempered princess. Nobody seemed to like her, which was evident in the way her guards handled her, and even the woman in charge of her seemed to despise the princess, only wishing to maintain her position as her guardian a while longer for appearance sake, no doubt. Which confirmed Mirabella was a terror.

Why hide her away? Was it to keep her out of the clutches of greedy men, none of whom the king wanted her to wed? With her contemptible disposition, she would find no husband who would give her room to act poorly toward the staff, if the man had any backbone at all. Certainly, *he* wouldn't permit her to give his staff any grief and would lock her in a tower if she said one unkind word to the lowest of his servants.

"Why were you living at Mayden Castle?" he asked, stifling the correct protocol to call her princess. Her kind hadn't earned the privilege of their class. As a knight before he'd been crowned king, he'd learned to be chivalrous and kind to those who were in need. He couldn't quash the contempt he felt for her, and every other woman or man like her who used their title and privilege to their advantage, hurting those who served them in the process.

She didn't answer him.

Unused to insubordination, he was having a devil of a time remembering he was a knight as well as a king, and that he needed to keep his temper in check. Despite this, he growled, "Answer me now!"

She tilted her chin up higher and pursed her lips.

Grabbing her reins, he pulled her horse to a stop. "Would you prefer walking?" Not that he wanted her to walk. They would never get anywhere, and he imagined she'd blister her feet and be a mess. But maybe walking would knock some of the willfulness out of her.

She glared at him; her brown eyes flickered with a red-hot flame. "You can bully me all you like, Your Grace," she hissed. "But know this, there is only one man I fear and it is my uncle. So do your worse." She whipped her head around and stared straight ahead.

For a moment, Leogane glowered at her in stunned silence. He had no idea what to say to her. No one spoke in such a manner to him. Come to think of it, not even his enemies when captured would speak to him thus. The idea grated on him that she was right. There was very little he could do to her to make her talk. But he wondered, as fearless as she appeared, and it didn't seem to be a show, why she would fear her uncle.

Leogane released her reins and motioned for her to continue walking her horse beside him. "If you think you will anger me enough to give you up to Vladek, think again."

She glanced at him, her look bewildered.

Instantly, he wondered why he'd even said what he did, now having no intention of making the witch his wife.

Once they'd gone a short distance into the Larimar Forest, Mirabella tightened her hands around her reins, making her knuckles turn white. Her face lost all its color, and her brown eyes searched for signs of something in the surrounding woods.

He hadn't heard or seen anything, nor had his men indicated

anything was the matter. "What ails you? Did you hear or see anything amiss?" he asked, wondering if she was afraid of the woods.

"I've...I've never traveled through this forest before. I...I hear all kinds of strange sounds."

He gave a short bark of laughter to which she responded with a sharp glance of resentment. "Sorry, my lady," he said, mocking the prim, proper princess who'd never ventured out of the castle, too afraid to muddy the hems of her gowns, he suspected. "I hadn't realized you'd never left the grounds of your castle."

"I have never left the tower," she replied curtly, her blond brows furrowed, her mouth pinched in annoyance.

He laughed again. "Worse even still." Then he studied her, though she quickly turned her face away. "You are not one of those souls who are afraid to venture beyond your chamber, are you?" He'd heard of people like that, who were so mortified of what lay beyond their room, they lived and died there, never having ventured forth their entire lives. He could not have a wife like that, who would need to help run his staff, and keep the castle in good order when he and his men went to battle.

"Why would you desire to wed me when you know so little about me?" she asked.

"I do *not* desire to wed you."

The scowl returned to her face, and she looked away, but her question made him think she hadn't had a choice about staying in her chamber. Had her uncle worried men would gain access to her, if she hadn't been well hidden away? On the other hand, was it that she'd tried to escape her uncle's rule?

Now that created new lumps in his porridge. If the lady was that willful...

Again, he shook his head, wondering how he'd gotten himself into this mess. "Why, pray tell, did you stay in your chamber?" He might as well ask, though he was not sure he would hear the truth when she gave him her version.

At first, she didn't answer, and he knew she was testing his resolve again, but then she turned her ear toward the north, and he thought he heard something too. Something ominous. Like before when he and his men had been attacked.

A flock of birds flew into the trees from the same direction, and Leogane shouted, "Form a circle around the women!" His heart thundered against his ribs as he pulled his sword from its scabbard. He was not afraid for himself or his men, but he worried about having the women in their midst. It could make fighting more difficult.

"What is it?" Mirabella asked.

"We were attacked by men three times on the journey here. I believe they were some of Count Vladek's men."

"How could you say such a thing? Accuse an innocent man of wrongdoing just—"

"Silence, woman!"

Blinking her eyes, she stared at him.

"They wore a crest on the tunics covering their chain mail. 'Twas the same as what my people said Vladek wore when he visited your uncle."

She licked her lips and swallowed hard.

He wasn't sure she believed him, and truly, he shouldn't have cared. It bothered him just the same that she would defend this Count Vladek whom she didn't know, according to her uncle. Unless...

Unless the villain had sneaked into the castle to see her before.

He couldn't think of that now, as his men circled around them. Leogane stayed close to the women, watching for any signs of an ambush.

For what seemed like an eternity, no one moved. The

princess's horse nickered softly, one of his men's horses snorted and pawed the ground uneasily, but it was Mirabella's face that revealed the first of the onslaught. Her eyes grew big, her lips quavered and she opened her mouth to cry out well before the enemy was even in sight. He didn't have any time to dwell on her strange actions as fifty or sixty men charged them, wearing black tunics emblazoned with a blood red rose.

As before, the men were good, but not strong enough for his men. It was like they were unused to battling on horseback, unlike his men who jousted when not in battle, and fought on their horses unless they were unseated. They'd grown up in the saddle, and every one of them fought as valiantly as before, delving blow after blow, swords clanking, horses prancing, and charging, circling and backing up, decimating the enemies' larger force.

Their enemies' faces were shielded by helmets, and again, Leogane wondered if any of these men were Vladek, though he assumed the count waited in hiding, expecting his men to deliver the princess to him instead, the coward that he was.

Leogane held his position in the inner circle, wanting to help his fellow knights fight the enemy, but forcing himself to remain beside the women in case any of the enemy broke through the outer circle.

The only method that seemed to kill the enemy was lopping off their heads; cuts to the arms or legs didn't slow them down much and attempting to penetrate their chain mail to reach their hearts was nigh to impossible. Yet, one of his greatest lancers had taken a lance and speared one of their enemy in an earlier battle and successfully killed the brigand. And an archer had managed to pierce the chainmail covering a knight's chest with a crossbow's bolt.

When the last of the men lay dead, and his own men raised

their swords in triumph, Leogane looked over at Mirabella and saw her face as gray as granite.

"They're not real," she said, her voice hushed.

"They're very real," Leogane assured her, and motioned for one of his knights to remove the helmet from a decapitated head.

When the knight lifted the helmet off the ground, a pile of dust poured out.

"What the..." Leogane stared at the empty helm. "Check the rest."

Not only had the heads disappeared, the bodies themselves had disintegrated into dust.

"Magic users," one of the men said, cursing. His brown eyes hot with hatred, he turned to Leogane. "Black magic."

"They're not dead," Mirabella whispered, tears clogging her throat.

"They're dead," Leogane reassured her, hoping to stay his men's concerns as well. He didn't need panic on his hands. They'd never bothered to check the other men they'd killed, leaving them for their lord to recover and bury, not wishing to delay their journey in the inhospitable woods.

"They're dead," he said again, and motioned for his men to move out. "Are you going to be all right, Princess?"

She nodded, but she didn't look well.

"A cottage is located a couple of miles ahead. A healer's hut. We'll stop there and you ladies can rest." Though he wished it not, as the stop would delay their journey overmuch.

"Thank you," she said, but the fight was no longer in her words, and he wondered if the lady truly was a recluse and the journey and fighting were too much for her. He'd never considered she might die on the journey, too frail to manage.

"Have you ever met this Count Vladek?" he asked, hoping to get her mind off the battle, if that's what still distressed her.

She stared at him with the oddest look, as if she didn't quite know the answer to his question. Was she in shock?

"Princess Mirabella, have you ever personally met the man at Castle Mayden?"

She shook her head and pulled her gaze away from his.

However, there was something she wasn't telling him, something that bothered her, and subsequently bothered him more than anything. What was she hiding?

6

Rina had wanted to join Leogane in the battle against the dark arts knights, but she was having her own fight while she'd been trying to slip in to tell the king she was Mirabella's protector. Ten men against one warrior elf? No trouble. She'd leapt off her horse and commanded him to run away as soon as she'd heard the men on horseback coming and she'd been caught between the forces that were attacking the king's men and the ones still coming. She didn't send Midnight back home, not just yet. Just out of range of the dark arts knights, their hideous faces masked. They'd been conjured up by a dark arts druid. She knew because she'd fought them before. And that time, she'd even killed the druid. Well, and two more times she'd had to deal with them—terminally, but it wasn't necessary to tell about *all* her heroics.

Thankfully, her magical ability had worked. But she'd had to catch them off-guard. Some called her the "Dark Arts Druid Slayer," but she detested the name. It made it sound as though that's all she did. Like being a dragon slayer. She was a warrior and with that came all kinds of responsibilities. Not just killing a few dark arts druids who threatened elf kind.

She blended into the tree bark when another knight tried to skewer her. His sword missed her by inches, but he couldn't see or hear her. She just hadn't moved away from her position quickly enough when she had cloaked herself in the appearance of the bark. Then she leapt into the air with her sword raised, landing on the back of the man's steed, and cut off the knight's head. Who said she should fight fair? There were still five against, well, four against one warrior elf.

His helmet fell to the ground, no body, just dust left behind as she shoved the rest of his armor and clothes off his horse and swung around to decapitate another of the knights. Once she'd beheaded him, she leaned down against the horse, hugging his neck and the beautiful black mane that whipped about in the breeze, another of the knights staring at the riderless horse, appearing puzzled. As soon as the knight was close enough to the horse, she rose up and swung her sword at him, beheading yet another of the knights. Three more to go. They were as persistent as she was at finishing the job.

Two came at her then, and she slid off to the side of the horse, blending in so they couldn't see her. They both swung their swords over the body of the horse, having no idea where she was, but assuming she was hiding on his back like she'd done before. Give her some credit! Once nothing happened, they watched the horse for what seemed an eternity, when she wanted to go to the princess's aid. But she figured she was already doing that by eliminating more of the dark art knights before they even reached Leogane's men.

Once the knights began to move off, probably assuming she had left the scene or was mortally wounded or dead, she moved back into the saddle and rode after the closest knight, beheaded him, and swiftly took after the other. He swung around, ready to kill her, but she had more important things to do and today wasn't her day to die. She struck his sword against hers, sending a metal clanking sound reverberating through the woods. She was torn about alerting Leogane's men that she was fighting the dark arts knights—if they saw what she could do—maybe they'd believe her useful, but what if they thought she was just as dangerous as the knights fighting Leogane's men?

But she couldn't fight this dark arts knight like she wanted to. She couldn't lop off his head like she'd tried to do. She realized she was getting tired. Then a bolt flew through the air, whizzing past her head and struck the dark knight in the back. Then another winged through air striking his helmed head. The archer wasn't fighting fair either, but against the dark arts creatures, anything that would take them down was the right way to do this.

The dark arts knight fell from his horse and landed on the ground, and Leogane's knightly archer pointed his crossbow in her direction. Yet there was one more dark arts knight who was unaccounted for.

She considered—vanishing. But then she wouldn't be able to use her ability in a more elusive way. She didn't like to give up her secrets to just anyone. They might fear she was just as dangerous as the dark arts knights were. Then again—she glanced around at the knights she'd dispatched—she was.

"We are fighting the same enemy," she said, trying not to sound annoyed that he was threatening her.

"Who are you, and why are you here?" the knight asked.

"I am Rina, a warrior elf, cousin to Dracolin, Warrior Chief of the shadow elves." Most elves knew of him and respected him, so it didn't hurt to use his title to elevate her own. "I'm here to protect Princess Mirabella." She motioned to the remnants of clothes and armor on the ground. "As you can see, I have done so. Who are you?"

"Artur, knight champion and archer, protector of the innocent and meek, King Leogane's trusted champion, and a friend of Dracolin's."

She arched a brow. She'd never heard of Artur before. Not that she made many courtly appearances, and certainly in the line of work she did, she rarely got to see Dracolin, so she had no idea who some of his friends were.

"He has never mentioned you," Artur said.

She smiled. "He has never mentioned he knows you either." So we're even, she wanted to say. "Well, Artur, take me to your leader then."

"You may not like what he has to say."

She sighed. "Take me or leave me. I will fight these dark arts knights on my own and protect all of you then."

ARTUR THOUGHT the warrior elf was the most beautiful creature he'd ever seen. He'd watched her behead the knight—what had she called it? A dark arts knight?—and readied herself to fight the last of the knights when he had dispatched the man, or whatever it was, for her instead. He couldn't let her have all the fun. Besides, some part of his knightly persona called on him to be chivalrous and save the woman, even if she hadn't needed saving. Still, how could he know that she hadn't needed his help? She had already slain most of the villains and one mistake could have cost her life. He didn't want to think that he did it to prove to her how good an archer he was though.

He couldn't see how she could eliminate so many of them, all on her own, just one lone warrior elf. He knew they were powerful, or at least he had heard wild tales about them, and thought they were just the stuff of legends. To actually witness one in combat, that was a real sight. But was she here to protect the princess or were her intentions other than honorable? She hadn't come to them before this to offer her services. She hadn't been at the castle protecting the princess there. Rina was an—enigma—to his way of thinking.

He rode with her to join Leogane where the king would have her explain her role more clearly.

"You are good with the crossbow," she finally said, riding the dark arts knight's mount.

"You are good with a sword. Did you come on foot?" He couldn't imagine how she could have come from the castle and kept up with them. But maybe that was another of her special talents. A fast and quiet runner.

"My horse is off that way. I had him leave me so he wouldn't be injured by the dark arts knights."

"He is not trained for combat then?"

"He is. But he is indispensable. I would not risk his life when I am fighting for my own."

He pondered that for a moment, thinking that a knight without a horse would be at a disadvantage in battle. But she wasn't a knight. "Do all warriors like yourself protect their mounts as you do?"

"I would hope so. They are excellent transportation and great companionship."

"Because you go it alone." That's what Artur had heard about them, anyway.

"When it takes only one warrior to get the job done? Aye." She frowned at him. "Why are you out here alone?"

"I came to investigate the sword fight I thought I'd heard. Leogane and the others are on their way to the healer's hut."

"Have some of your people been wounded?"

"Nay, but the princess was looking unwell and he was taking her there. If you"—he paused, thinking to ask her why she hadn't been at the castle, but maybe she had come from another direction and had just learned the princess was no longer there

—"weren't at the castle, how did you come to be here? And who hired you to protect the princess? Her uncle, the king? Someone else?" He couldn't imagine it would be the count, if the dark arts knights had been sent by him.

"Sometimes we are hired. Sometimes we hear rumors about situations that are wrong that need to be righted. In this case, I'd heard tales about a princess locked in a tower. Against her will? I had to investigate."

"And you found?"

"She was. She claims her uncle murdered her father."

Artur considered Rina's words. Leogane had said nothing to him or his advisor about this, and he hadn't heard anything about it either through courtiers' gossip. He wondered if the warrior was wrong—or if she was correct. He wondered, if Leogane already knew, or if not, and the story was true, what he would do. He was a fair sort of man, but he could be ruthless when he needed to be.

"You didn't know?" Rina asked, as if she knew for sure that the deed had been done, when she'd just said she'd come here to see for herself if any of this was true.

The princess's uncle had told Leogane to watch out for the princess's lies. That she could be very convincing. Leogane had warned his men about it, so they wouldn't be taken in by the princess's mistruths.

"Her uncle says she lies."

"Her uncle would."

Artur realized the warrior could be right. If the uncle had murdered Mirabella's father, and she had witnessed it, the easiest way to silence her was to lock her in a tower and tell everyone of import that the princess did not speak the truth. Who would believe the princess over the king?

"Do you believe her then?" Artur asked.

"I believe that she should be heard and not locked in a tower to keep her from voicing her concerns. I didn't have time to speak with her for very long before Leogane took her on this journey."

"So you were there when we first arrived?" Now that surprised Artur, having thought Rina had missed seeing the princess at the castle and had met up with them on the road. So where had she been? And why hadn't she been with the princess the whole time—if she was supposed to protect her. None of it made any sense.

"I had been there, but I couldn't reach the princess after that. Once I had my horse, I hurried to catch up to the party, heard the fighting on the road, but before I could help, I was attacked in the woods."

"You were not traveling on the road? It would have taken less time. You would have caught up with us sooner." That didn't make any sense either.

"It is a warrior's way. Do you know how many times travelers are waylaid by robbers on a road?"

"Often. But we are heavily armed knights."

"But I wasn't with you at the time. I was trying to catch up to you. So I would have been on the road alone."

He glanced back in the direction where she had successfully beaten the dark arts knights.

She nodded. "I avoid the roads and eliminate them, if necessary, out in the woods where they are hiding, ready to attack the unsuspecting traveler. I don't wear the heavy armor that knights wear. I have to protect myself in the best way I can."

'Twas true Mirabella had never been outside her chamber before, except when she'd managed to escape, but only to be caught on the first floor of the castle, and 'twas true she wasn't used to all the strange sounds of the forest, but there was something more to Mirabella's distress than that. She'd heard whispered words when no one else had seemed to hear them. She heard the men scouting up ahead speaking to each other from time to time, joking with each other about her unsuitability to their lord, betting whether he would wed her or his advisor's daughter.

Her stomach grew cold with the notion. For too many years she'd lived in veritable isolation, but being with people now did not improve her life. She'd wanted to escape her captivity, but most of all, she wanted to right a wrong, to punish her uncle for murdering her father and stealing the crown, to rule the kingdom herself, not like the tyrant he was, but as a good ruler like she'd overheard their people say her father had been.

It seemed an impossibility. She hadn't wanted the aggressors to slay her escort, yet she had not wanted the "enemy" killed either. She'd sworn that the count had whispered her name, saying he wanted her and desired to bring her home to her mother's people.

Glancing at Leogane, she found him watching her. He seemed concerned for her welfare, which dissolved some of her animosity for him.

The savage fighting hadn't bothered her as much as the whispered words that had filled her head, or the strange fact that her hearing seemed to be growing more sensitive by the day. It made her think she was losing her mind.

Closing her eyes, she listened to a mammal lapping at a stream nearby, and heard a bird of prey whoosh down to the forest floor, snatching a squeaking mouse in its wicked talons. When she opened her eyes, she expected to see the mammal and the bird, but neither were anywhere in sight. She had never had this acute sense of hearing before either, not until a few nights ago.

At first, she had ignored it, or tried to.

But when she'd stood at her window back at Mayden Castle, she'd even begun to hear the soldiers complain about how boring their jobs were while they surveyed the surrounding land from the wall walk encircling the inner bailey. Even on still days when there was no breeze to carry their voices. Even on windy days when the air circulated well away from the castle. Was it a magic user's gift? Was it because she was nearly twenty?

She heard no more whispers in the woods, other than the low talking of some of their escort, some fearing the enemy were magic users. A ripple of chills cascaded down her arms and she pulled her black cloak tighter.

The last time she'd ridden a horse she had been seven. Riding the horse seemed easy enough, and the four-legged beast seemed to take to her at once. The first critter she'd ever had the chance to befriend. She'd never even been allowed to pet the dogs in the great hall. She wondered if she might be able to win Justina over now that the girl was no longer under Phiri's or the guards' influence. She needed an ally, no matter who the person was. She'd heard fighting off in the woods and thought it possibly was Rina and her force of warriors. She prayed if it was, they were uninjured during the battle.

Once they stopped at the healer's hut—as it seemed the king intended for Mirabella to ride at his side until that time—she would speak to the girl and find out all she could about her uncle's court and attempt to make friends with her.

She glanced at the king and observed him further. Despite the scar that ran across his cheek, she found him to be a handsome man, though he was far too irritating to be her husband. Not only that, she would never agree to be any man's wife who was devoted to serving her uncle. The king turned to look at her, and she quickly looked away, her cheeks heating.

He scoffed. "It seems your cheeks are no longer a sickly gray, but have a rosy color to them now, my lady."

"'Tis the chill in the air, Your Grace."

"Ah. You have not told me why you remained in your chamber."

Glaring at him, she said, "You are the king's loyal vassal. You serve him whether he has done wrong or not. Would it matter to you what he has done to me? To my father? You will agree that he had just cause, or not believe me at all."

Leogane stared at her in surprise, but for several minutes didn't respond. Was it because he was a king himself and didn't like to hear her say what she truly thought of him? Or he was being careful to choose the proper words in response? Either that or he thought she was a liar. Then her heart sank. Her uncle would say as much about her, because once she was released from her prison, she would tell the world about her mistreatment. He couldn't afford to have a vassal lord suddenly turn on him to seek vengeance for his wife's abuse and her father's murder.

"No matter what I say, you will not believe me."

For a moment, he didn't reply. Then finally, he nodded and looked away.

That hurt worse than the time her uncle took a handful of rushes to her back, angered because she'd called him a murderer, whipping her until she had passed out. She would never submit to her uncle. Never apologize for what she knew in her heart was true.

She longed for someone to care about her, to avenge her father's death, but Leogane would never be that man.

I care, the wind whispered, the sound darkly seductive, strangely close, yet far away. She whipped her head around and saw nothing. She knew then she was losing her mind. Unless it was the warrior elf who had come to her tower room to aid her.

_____

7

As Rina and Artur rode their horses to see King Leogane, she knew she had to help the princess so that she could make her own choices in life. She just hoped there wasn't a whole lot of bloodshed over this. She was all about helping those who needed help, obtaining peace without bloodshed if she could, but she knew a dark wind had been blowing this day and something evil was in the works.

She thought it didn't have anything to do with King Leogane, but with the other—the one who wanted Mirabella but would send his men to kill King Leogane and his knights. Someone in the shadows, striking at the heart of the princess's escort. Rina had to side with someone, beyond just the princess, if they were to win this battle.

And Rina was staking her life on Leogane.

Rina heard the men on horseback approaching Leogane's men and she needed to take a stand—again. Artur, who was riding nearby her, shouted to the king and his men in the distance, "They are coming!"

She was afraid that these new knights might win against Leogane's one of these times, and she wouldn't be able to rescue the princess. She moved in quickly to kill the first of the men. She was certain they were created by a dark arts druid. To kill them, they had to remove their heads or pierce their hearts. Doing anything less to them would be fruitless. She leapt to a tree branch onto the back of one of the aggressor's horses and removed the knight's head before he could cry out. Then she rode after another as she heard Leogane's men call out, repeating what Artur had already said, that more of the enemy was coming.

She swung her sword at the next of the men as she quickly rode up on him, the rest of the dark arts knights believing the riderless horse was just running with them. She had to use rene-gade tactics against such a force and it certainly worked for her. She beheaded him and rode toward the next one maneuvering around the branches of a tree and did the same to him, lopping his head off and he fell to the ground. His helmet rolled away from his head and all that was left of his head was dust.

Thankfully, Artur was making his own impact on slaying the knights.

Then there were only two more left, but bolts from Leogane's archers' crossbows struck the last two aggressors in the heart and they fell.

"I am with the princess!" Rina shouted, hoping that Leogane's men didn't shoot her on sight. She was riding one of the attacker's horses with the saddle that was just the same as the others. "I killed the others that were coming to attack you!" Well and Artur assisted, but he could make his own claims.

"She's with me," Artur said, surprising her.

"She's with me," the princess shouted, looking grateful that Rina had arrived to aid her.

"Who are you?" the king asked, allowing her to join them, but a couple of his men still had swords ready in the event she wasn't who she professed to be.

"Rina, warrior shadow elf of a long line of warrior elves, cousin to Dracolin, Warrior Chief. I'd learned the princess had been imprisoned at her uncle's castle and had come to free her."

"It's true, she did," the princess said.

Artur was beside Rina, not disputing what she said, just listening in.

"Who do you work for?" the king asked, his eyes narrowed. He didn't believe her, not that she was surprised. She had come in behind two of the enemy knights and hadn't appeared to be with the princess. If she was, why hadn't she been with her from the beginning?

"No one. When I heard the rumors, I had to learn if it was true. Which I did discover was the truth. Then you came along and messed up my whole plan."

The king smiled. "You and who else?"

"No one else. Sometimes it's easier to slip in and slip away with the person you're aiding, rather than bringing a huge show of force."

"True."

"She's with us," Artur repeated. "At least she's not against us. She has killed several of these knights already."

"Aye, and I'm here to protect the princess further. Do you know who these men work for?" Rina asked.

"Vladek as far as we know. We were attacked en route to pick up the princess. Where had you intended to take her, had you made it out of the tower before we arrived?" the king asked her as they began to ride along the road again.

"To my home, my village. My family would have helped to protect her until we could right the wrong done to her."

"And you know this for certain?" Leogane looked like he wasn't sure what to believe.

"Aye. She was locked in the tower and no one was there to protect her. Do you think that ogre of a woman had been?"

"No. You're right. She only wanted the position because she thought she could gain by it. But she would never have had a place in my household," the king said.

Rina eyed the other woman with suspicion, then leaned over close to the king and said low for his ears only, "Do you trust the maid?"

"I had."

"I do not. She was someone the princess's uncle hired. No one whom he paid should be trusted."

"And me?" the king asked, looking amused.

"I don't know. Are you trustworthy?" Rina did not kowtow to royalty. He could be just as much of a beast as the princess's uncle was. Rina whistled and one of his men raised his sword, looking ready to kill her. "I'm calling to my horse. I left him behind so I could take out the last man in the line of brigands, and ride his horse in. Then my horse was safe and the men in front of him wouldn't hear the sound of a different horse or two instead of just the one."

"You are a warrior." Leogane acted as though he realized that's just what she was.

"Just as I said."

"Since you have no job, no earnings to take on this mission of protecting the princess, I hereby hire you to do so," Leogane said.

Rina didn't want to take a bribe from someone who might be just as rotten as the princess's uncle, yet she couldn't turn down honest money, if that's what this truly was. She had to pay the shadow elf King Sar's taxes no matter what she was paid to do. "I accept." She turned in the saddle and smiled to see her horse coming to join them. "That's my horse. You may have this one in case someone's horse is killed in a future battle. It seems as though we will have more of these knights to fight. Did you realize that you would have trouble like this?"

"No, I hadn't believed so." Leogane turned to speak to Artur. "You are friends with Dracolin. Do you know Rina?"

Artur glanced at her and looked as though he wished he could say yes, though that could just be her imagination. Being loyal to his king, which was what she would expect of him, Artur shook his head.

"Which is to be expected," Rina said. "Dracolin and I don't get to see each other all that much, what with the jobs we do. And now that he is married to the langolar, even more so. Have you met her, Your Grace? She is unusual, to say the least."

The king smiled a little at Rina, and she suspected he thought the same of her because she had one blue eye and one green. Rina was ready to fight anyone who would attempt to ruin her mission to save the princess, but for now, it behooved her to make an alliance of sorts with Leogane until she determined it worked against her plans.

MIRABELLA WASN'T sure what was going on with Rina and couldn't believe she'd arrived here all on her own. Maybe her companions were hiding in the woods, waiting for Rina's order to steal Mirabella away. Everyone had heard of Dracolin, and she had to admire Rina for being related to the great shadow elf Warrior Chief. It seemed Rina had some of his fighting skills also.

The king looked at the man he'd called Artur, his champion of knights, and he inclined his head in silent agreement. What had just passed between them? Then Mirabella realized Artur was riding next to Rina, who rode ahead of them with more men in front of them. So was Artur watching Rina, ready to strike her down if he thought she was not who she said she was?

Mirabella was certain that was the case.

Later that day, they arrived at the healer's hut. Leogane hadn't spoken another word to Mirabella, and she'd been just as grateful. If they came under attack by Vladek's men, she would stay with the party, as long as Rina was watching out for her. For now, she had every intention of speaking to Justina, but Leogane pulled Mirabella from her horse and guided her into the thatched one-room house without a word.

Then he posted guards at the windows and door and headed back outside.

The king said to the maid, "You come with me."

"Send Justina inside with me," the princess said, furious that the king would stop her from speaking with her maid. Everyone seemed to conspire against her. She wanted to know if she could make friends with her now that she was no longer under her guardian's control.

But he didn't listen to her or respond.

RINA SUSPECTED the king wanted to learn the truth—was Justina on the princess's side, or her uncle's? She figured the woman was a spy for the princess's uncle. She glanced at Artur who was keeping an eye on Rina, not on the princess.

"Do you mind if I go inside the healer's hut also?" Normally Rina would have just done so, but she felt she was walking a fine line here.

"Aye. I'll go with you," Artur said. At least he didn't have to ask the king's permission for her to join Mirabella.

"Would you like some mead, my lady?" the healer asked Mirabella. The black-haired woman was standing over a kettle, stirring some bubbling liquid. Curls of blue mist rose from the frothing liquid. Her mouth curved up and the warmth reached all the way to her sparkling amber eyes. "Mead, my lady," the woman asked again. She appeared youthful, maybe in her early twenties, yet her voice and actions seemed much older.

"Thank you," Mirabella said.

"But she has her own flask to drink from," Rina quickly said.

Mirabella looked surprised that Rina would jump in and stop her from accepting the healer's generosity. "She's...right. Do you hear much news here about the surrounding region?"

"People come through here from time to time, aye," the woman said and motioned to a wooden chair beside a small round table. "Have a seat. What is it you wish to know?"

"Do you know anything about Count Vladek?" Mirabella asked, still standing.

The woman's lips curved up even more. "He is a handsome man, about the same age as your king."

"He is *not* my king."

Smiling more broadly, the woman nodded, and went back to stirring her broth, or whatever it was.

Artur was standing in the doorway, his arms folded across his chest, looking commanding.

"What is your name? I'm afraid I've been locked up forever in the tower and don't have any gift for your hospitality—"

"You have many gifts, my lady. You will soon learn to use them."

"I'm a magic user?" Mirabella quickly asked, then glanced at Rina and Artur as if she made a mistake in asking the healer in front of the others.

The woman's dark brows rose.

"Not a magic user? Then what?"

"Your mother was from Racine."

"Where Count Vladek is from?"

"Aye. I am Sistenia and have to tell you that you must not wed Leogane if you wish to put matters right with your uncle."

"You know? You know how poorly my uncle treated me? That he killed my father? Tell the king for me! Be my witness!"

"Leogane cares not what befell your father or you. Just like your uncle, he's a greedy man."

Artur cleared his throat, reminding the healer he was here with the king, and he didn't appreciate her words.

The healer sighed. "He doesn't want you, and yet he has removed you from Castle Mayden. Why? Because he wants the lands and coin that King Inari will bestow upon him. He is the king's first choice. Leogane will take you as a wife, and maybe you will suffer an accident? He will then marry his chief advisor's daughter, the woman he already loves, and have your properties too."

Rina glanced at Artur, looking to see if that was so. He wouldn't meet her gaze so she suspected it was true.

Mirabella took a sip of her wine from her flask. "What about Count Vladek? Would he not gain much by marrying me?"

"He has already told King Inari he doesn't want anything but you. You are of Racine bloodlines. You belong with your people."

Rina thought that appealed to Mirabella. Belonging someplace with her own people. People that would care about her. Sounded inviting. Yet, Rina still couldn't set aside the feeling that Count Vladek may very well have had his men attempt to kill her escort and take her by force. But maybe that was the only way he'd be able to have her, because Leogane already was the king's first choice.

"I don't want Count Vladek's men to attack my escort. I don't want to see any more of *his* men die either."

Sistenia didn't say anything, just stirred the contents of her pot.

"Can you get word to him?"

The woman's lips turned up. "Aye."

"Will he...will he listen."

"It's difficult to say. He wishes to please you, but he also wants you. He feels no one will take care of you like one of your own kind."

Rina suspected no one had ever wanted to please the princess, nor had anyone wanted her, and the notion had to appeal to her. But the healer was definitely siding with Vladek, and Rina didn't trust her. She was surprised Artur didn't take the healer to task for what she was saying about Leogane, even if it was true.

Rina suspected the king had no plan to let her take the princess to her home either. He would believe his castle would protect her better. And he could be right. But would he fight on the princess's behalf to help her get rid of her uncle? Free the people from his tyranny? If they discovered he truly was a tyrant, not caring a thing about the people, only about the rich and powerful that he kept at his beck and call. Should any of them disappoint him, would he throw them to the wolves, so to speak?

"Have you ever seen people such as these that Leogane's men have been fighting?" Rina asked the healer.

"Such as?"

"The men who die and leave dust behind?"

The healer shook her head.

There was something not quite right about the healer, Rina thought. She didn't even act surprised that men died and turned to dust. What was up with that? She had eyed Rina's sword thrice already and Rina didn't think the woman should worry about her being a warrior unless she had some reason to worry. Rina moved the princess farther away from the healer and her bubbling black cauldron, just in case she had to protect her. "Have you been here long?" Rina asked the woman.

"Aye, for years."

Rina looked at the princess for confirmation. She shook her

head. "I've never been out of the castle, not since I was taken there when I was seven."

Rina had hoped she could confirm that the woman was who she appeared to be. Or not to be, as Rina feared. "You've never encountered these creatures before?" Rina asked the woman again.

"I have said no, have I not?"

Rina smiled. "Aye, but, well, they seemed to know you." Which was totally made up, but if she got a rise out of the woman, she could tell if she was in league with them or not.

The woman gave her a smile that didn't reach her eyes. "I have never seen them before. I'm sure word has gotten out that I'm the healer for the region."

"Aww, but what could you do for them when they turn to dust? I mean, they don't appear to need a healer once they are injured."

"I wouldn't know, though I'm sure if they live in this area at all, the word would have reached them about me."

"Uh-huh." Which was true, and the woman was careful not to react in any way that said otherwise. But it still didn't explain how the healer could live here without encountering them. Rina still didn't trust the woman. Suffice it to say, she did have trust issues. Some of that was due to her boyfriend cheating on her right before she came on this mission. So it wasn't that she was just jaded.

"Do you want something to drink?" the healer asked Rina.

This time Rina gave her a smile that was just as insincere. She patted her flask at her hip. "I'm good but thank you for the generous offer." She probably put the sweet sarcasm on a little thickly, but she was a warrior, not a politician. "Do you know Healer Xanadu?"

She was the healer in Rina's neck of the woods and most healers knew of each other, since this wasn't that far from home.

Though that wasn't her name exactly. It was Xander, but the healer should pick up on that right away.

The healer frowned. "I'm not sure. It sounds like someone I should know, but it doesn't sound quite right somehow."

Okay, Rina could give her that. She was awful with names herself. Still, she didn't trust the woman.

The door squeaked open, and a guard walked inside. "His Grace wished me to stay inside with the lady also."

The healer turned her head a little and nodded. "As you wish."

Sinking onto the hard-wooden chair, Mirabella sipped from her own flask farther away from the healer.

8

Two of Leogane's men gathered wood for a campfire while others caught game for the meal. The rest kept watch while Leogane spoke to Justina. "Tell me about your mistress."

Justina looked back at the hut, as if she were afraid to tell the truth.

His jaw tightened; he couldn't abide by anyone being cruel to servants. "You have nothing to fear from the lady. Please tell me what she's like."

"Why she is cruel, my lord. She pulled the wings off a baby bird, and killed the poor thing afterwards. She pushed a young boy into a swollen river, and no one could save him before he drowned. She loves nothing, man or beast. Even when governesses would try to teach her anything, she would throw such fits her tutors quit. She has started fires in the castle, escaped so many times that she has to be guarded always. And, I hate to say this about the princess, but..." The woman looked at the ground, and bit her lip, then looked up at Leogane. "Everyone knows she makes up any story she can to suit herself. She blames others for her actions too."

He nodded sympathetically, then crossed his arms and took a deep breath. "Yet you seemed relieved you were leaving Castle Mayden. If it meant serving the lady further, why is this so?"

"That place is a horrible castle to stay at. You saw the way it was, isolated from the rest of the world like a giant prison."

"Was the lady imprisoned in the tower for very long?"

"I wouldn't know."

But she knew about everything else. It seemed odd she would not know about this. "Her father died in a hunting accident when she was seven. Was that when she was moved to the tower?" He wondered then if that was when the trouble began. A troubled child, angered her father was no longer king, or maybe because he'd died.

Before Justina could answer, Erlig, his chief advisor, hurried to speak with him, his face ashen, his posture concerned. "Your Grace," he said, "I must speak with you in private."

Leogane said to Justina, "Wait here for me. I have further questions."

She curtseyed deeply, smiling. "Aye, my lord, and I eagerly await your return."

Too eagerly, he thought.

Out of her hearing, he said, "What's the trouble Erlig?"

"We found the healer dead in the bushes several yards from the house. She's black haired like the woman inside, but I swear the woman we found dead is the healer, and the other, an imposter. The dead woman smelled of herbs normally used for healing potions. She had been gathering medicinal herbs in the woods and then storing them in a pouch attached to her belt."

Leogane pulled his sword, and so did Erlig and stormed to the hut. But then thinking better of it, he sheathed his sword, and motioned for his advisor to do the same. Carefully, he pulled the door open, and seeing the princess unharmed he said, "The boar is done. Come join us outside."

She should have done as he told her, but instead, she turned her head toward the campfire outside. "It doesn't smell done to me."

'Twas not the fact she acted contrary to his wishes that perturbed him so, but she seemed to sense things she ought not. Worse, if he didn't get her out of the hut at once before the imposter realized what he intended his men to do...

"I wish to speak with you in private, princess. Does it always have to be a contest of wills between us?" he asked, his voice on edge.

She rose slowly from the chair, and he imagined if she could do so even more slowly, she would. When she neared him, he seized her arm, ignoring her gasp, and pulled her out of the hut. He motioned to Erlig to enter, though Rina nodded to Leogane as if telling him he was doing the right thing.

As if he needed her to tell him he was. Already two more of his men were at his side, and the three rushed in, then slammed the door. With Artur in there also, and Rina, if she was trustworthy, they would question the healer and put an end to the imposter's life.

Leogane pulled the princess farther away from the hut, hoping the woman inside wouldn't shriek or that Mirabella wouldn't hear their swords cut the woman down. Had the imposter thought to poison him and his men? That's what he assumed.

"What...what's happening?" Mirabella asked, her face stricken.

He realized then, she would guess what was going on. "The woman was an imposter and murdered the real healer. My men found her dead in the bushes some distance from the hut." Though he hadn't expected the lady's brown eyes to roll back in her head, the color to drain from her cheeks so quickly, or her knees to buckle out from under her, he caught her as soon as she swooned. He couldn't help but notice the softness of her curves resting in his arms, or the sweet fragrance of rosewater that enveloped her like a floral fairy meadow. 'Twas unacceptable that he felt anything for the woman.

Taking his mind off the temptress, he wondered if the woman had no heart, felt nothing for man or beast, why had she fainted dead away? 'Twas not a trick either. He had seen women perform such faints to get his attention or other male admirer's, but in their cases, their cheeks remained the same color as before. He carried her to his bedding and lay her on the blankets next to the fire, caressing her hand and patting it, not sure what else to do.

"Is the lady all right?" Erlig asked, joining him.

"Aye. Is the witch dead?"

"Aye. But you won't believe what happened."

"What?"

"Jeremka stabbed her several times, missing her heart and the woman still didn't die. When Artur cut off her head, she turned to dust."

"She was one of them then. One of Count Vladek's people."

"Artur said aye. The imposter healer was telling the princess that she should go with Vladek. That he wasn't being paid to wed her like you were. There was something else, Your Grace." Erlig motioned to the princess. "Jeremka overheard the princess telling the healer to get in touch with Vladek."

"The princess was going to have all of us murdered in our sleep." Leogane was afraid the princess wasn't to be trusted so she could get her way, but this was going too far.

Erlig quirked a black brow and folded his arms. "Nay, the princess asked the woman to get a message to the count. Specifically, to tell him not to harm her escort."

"Not to harm us?" Leogane couldn't believe it. The woman

was cold blooded like Vladek's people if the maid's words were true.

"Her mother was from Racine. Did you know?"

The king stood. "She was a magic user?"

Erlig shrugged. "I don't know that everyone from there is. Maybe only the ones who are sent to thwart us and take the lady home with them. The imposter told the princess you wanted her lands, whereas the count wanted them not. He only wishes the lady because she belongs with her people."

Leogane did not believe the count one bit. Why would anyone give up the lady's lands when they were offered as her dowry? If Vladek wished her so badly, why had he not sought to take her earlier? Something about this stank, like a mongrel dog that had rolled in something dead.

"Anything else?"

"The imposter told the princess that you would take her for your wife, then she would meet with an accident, and you would then marry my daughter, the woman you truly love."

Shaking his head, Leogane paced. "I assume the princess believes it."

He had a mind to leave the woman behind for Count Vladek's minions to pick her up and take her to Racine, while the king returned home to his castle where the beautiful Callie awaited his warm embrace and wedded bliss.

Yet, things didn't add up. Why would the princess not want her escort killed, if she was a cold-blooded woman like the maid had said? He glanced over at the woman who watched them, her eyes big. She hadn't made a move toward them to help with her mistress.

Erlig looked back at her maid, apparently also wondering why the woman wasn't helping with the princess.

"Get me some water." Leogane crouched beside Mirabella.

He couldn't ignore the fact she'd tried to get word to the count's men not to harm them.

Erlig hurried back with a bucket of cold water, while his men either continued to cook the boar they had killed or served on guard duty.

Taking a cloth from his pack, the king wetted it and wiped the princess's face. Immediately she tried to sit up, but held her head and lay back down.

He watched her, noticing at once the color had not returned to her face. "Are you all right, princess?"

Her eyes filled with tears, and she looked away.

"She murdered the healer, my lady." Then he lied, figuring it was the truth, though he didn't know for certain. "She intended to poison us, all but you, before we bedded down for the night."

Mirabella closed her eyes, and tears dribbled down her cheeks.

He patted her hand, and stood. Was she upset her message would not get to Count Vladek? "The boar will be done soon, my lady. Then we'll sleep, and get an early start in the morn." He motioned to Erlig. "Watch her."

"Aye, Your Grace. Like a hawk." Erlig moved his pack to sit on beside her.

"Where is Artur?" Leogane asked.

"Speaking to the warrior elf, Rina."

"Good." Leogane hoped Artur could learn all he could about her.

When the meal was done, the princess would not eat, rolled onto her side, and pulled Leogane's blankets around herself. After he'd eaten, the king carried her inside the hut, and lay her in the bed.

Opening her eyes, she stared at him when he pulled the blanket up to her chin.

"You will sleep in here where it is more comfortable. There is only one bed, no sense in letting it go to waste. We will find no dwelling for the next night. Rina, Artur, Erlig, and your maid will stay inside with you to protect you."

She nodded and closed her eyes. The other knights took turns guarding the hut or sleeping outside.

Twice in the middle of the night, the princess cried out, the men grumbled, and Rina quieted her fears. Twice more she walked in her sleep, though at first he thought she was trying to escape, then realized she was sleepwalking like Leogane's sister did when she was overly tired at night.

The next morning, his men served porridge, and the party remounted for another day's journey, only this time Leogane intended to ride much longer, or at this rate, they'd never make it to Castle Grande.

Because the princess had such a restless night, she looked half asleep, her blond hair braided, but half of her silken tresses undone. She still seemed distraught, incapable of noticing she hadn't properly fixed her hair. Her maid never offered to help her. When he had looked in Rina's direction, she had thrown up her hands as if to say a warrior did not braid a princess's hair.

Mirabella had also waved away the morning meal.

Leogane glanced back at the maid, who watched the woods, probably fearing more attacks, but he couldn't help feeling annoyed that the woman, who was being paid to serve the princess, wasn't doing her job. When they stopped to eat later, he would insist she braid the princess's hair, and he wouldn't allow Mirabella to miss another meal.

For now, though, he kept his eye on the princess, who appeared ready to fall asleep at any moment. Twice she nodded off, and he reached out to wake her, not wanting her to fall from her horse and risk injury.

The third time, he reached over, and pulled her from her saddle, startling her.

"What—"

"You're falling asleep, and we can't afford to stop after we've only just begun our journey. Rest."

Jeremka rode up from behind, his blond hair flying, and he grabbed her horse's reins, then dropped back.

Artur and Rina rode side by side behind them, Erlig and the maid in front of them.

Mirabella sat stiffly in Leogane's arms for a good half hour, then slowly sank against him. The next thing he knew, her head was planted against his chest, and she was sleeping soundly. He told himself he had no feelings for the woman, yet he had never held a lady so close, and he couldn't help but enjoy the feel of her against his body, fitting nicely like the soft leather gloves he wore when he hunted with his bow.

Erlig rode up beside him. "She's like your mother was at night, eh?"

"Sleepwalking. Aye. The man who weds her will have to tie her to his bed if he wants her to remain there."

Erlig laughed. "I know you have an obligation to her uncle, and Callie understands this as well. Think nothing of it if you decide to take the princess for your wife."

Leogane took a deep breath. "I do not know what to think of the woman, but she is not the one for me. If she is a magic user, she should be with her people."

"If she is a magic user, why doesn't she use her powers?"

Leogane looked over at his advisor, realizing at once the gravity of the situation. "Did the healer imposter fight you?"

"No, it was as if she had been ordered to be a sacrificial lamb."

He shook his head. "I don't understand. Unless these people aren't magic users."

"Or unless they don't want to reveal their powerful use of magic, just yet."

"Something's not right. I can't pinpoint what, but something's not right." Leogane turned to his advisor. "When we were in the hut, could you smell if the boar was finished cooking?"

"I was making sure the imposter was killed."

"Aye."

"Why do you ask, Your Grace?"

Erlig had been his devoted advisor once the king's father had died from a fever. He trusted him with his life, never having kept any secrets from him, yet now, Leogane couldn't reveal what concerned him most about the lady. He shook his head. "'Tis nothing."

His advisor looked at the lady sleeping in the king's arms, and he was sure Erlig figured the lady was either some sort of sorcerer, or something they knew not what, just as he suspected.

Erlig looked ahead and waved his arm at the cliff faces banded in green, gold, and red strips of clay as if a master painter colored the whole cliffs in his spare time. "We are nearly to the pass."

"Aye, and I suspect they will attack us there again."

Jagged outcroppings of rocks covered with bushy fir trees provided perfect brigand hiding places, while they waited for the unsuspecting to travel through.

Leogane's scouts returned to the king to report before they ventured into the pass. "Your Grace," one of the men said. "We heard nothing. Shall we venture into the pass?"

Mirabella lifted her head from Leogane's chest and shook it. "Nay, they are waiting for us there." She pointed to the right of the pass. "Behind those rocks that look like my uncle's enormous beak."

His men stared at the princess in disbelief, and Leogane wondered the same thing. "How do you know this, my lady?"

"Did you not hear them?" she asked, her brows raised and her eyes wide with disbelief. "They were counting our numbers, having assumed you might have lost some of your men in the earlier battle. Did you not hear them?"

He didn't know what to think about her now. "Could you tell me how many there are?"

"Three, I think. Unless there are more who didn't speak. But I heard three distinctive voices."

"We can easily take them if there's only three of them," the scout said.

"What if she's wrong?" Erlig asked, his voice concerned.

What his advisor didn't say was what if the woman had lied?

"You, Artur, Rina, and Jeremka stay with the princess." Leogane would have included the maid, but he didn't fear that the maid would run away or that Vladek's men would care anything about her. "Guard her well." If he decided to turn the princess over to Vladek, he wanted it on his terms, not on hers. And he wanted to make sure Rina didn't slip off with the princess either.

"Aye, my lord." Erlig helped Mirabella from Leogane's horse, but instead of putting her on her own, he kept her on his saddle.

She objected at once. "Shouldn't—"

"I will protect you better this way."

Leogane nodded. His advisor knew his thoughts well without having to speak them. He motioned to the rest of his men. "I believe a force of at least three men are at that first outcropping of rocks to the right. We'll send them back to the devil from where they came."

With his sword raised, he led his men to battle, and hoped the lady had not sent them into a trap.

9

Artur knew his place was protecting the princess, though he wanted to remain with his king. He also knew Leogane wanted him to keep an eye on Rina, should she decide the princess and she would do better taking off on their own.

He listened for any trouble around him, as much as he wanted to watch straight ahead and see what his king was getting himself into. But since Artur was with the princess, he couldn't let his guard down in case they were set upon here.

"You suspected the healer was an imposter, Rina," Artur quietly said to her.

"Aye."

"How did you come to that conclusion?"

"She kept eyeing my sword. Her smiles were not genuine. But mainly because she didn't make any sense when she spoke to me about the men coming to see her if they needed healing when they disintegrated upon death into dust. If she knew of Vladek and seemed to be in touch with him, why wouldn't she also know about his men and their strange condition that would not require a healer? Also, because she was on Vladek's side."

Rina glanced at Artur. "Why did you not defend the king's honor?"

"It is for him to defend himself, and not up to me. He will get an alliance if he weds the lass and he will get a dowry, her lands, and money. So he has much to gain. The healer was right about that. But he would not kill the princess after he wed her. I figured everyone in the hut would assume the healer was lying about that so there was no need to defend the king. If the princess died, he could very well lose his alliance with her uncle, so why would he do that?" Artur shook his head. "King Leogane is the most honest of men."

SAID HIS LOYAL CHAMPION, Rina thought. Who was to say it wouldn't happen just the way the healer said? She glanced over at Mirabella who was watching the business with Leogane and his men. She seemed genuinely concerned for their welfare, not like she hoped he would be killed so she would be free of marrying him.

"Maybe I did see you once when I visited Dracolin," Artur said.

"You would have remembered me better than that." Rina knew she hadn't seen him.

"I saw this dark-haired elf dancing by herself when Dracolin married Persephonice," Artur said.

"You were at their wedding then?"

"Aye, but there were tons of people at the wedding. Persephonice is much loved by all. As is Dracolin." Artur glanced at Rina. "You had strings of feathers in your hair, and you were wearing a silver circlet."

She had been, so maybe he had been there and had seen her.

"Why were you dancing by yourself?" he asked.

"I wished to. There is no crime in that. What about you? I never saw you."

"I was visiting with the prince, who told me many a tale about Persephonice and how Dracolin's father and the king himself had forbidden Dracolin from seeing her further."

"Do you see what good that did?"

"Aye." Artur smiled. "When Dracolin's mind is made up, that is that."

"Do you ever wonder if any others of their kind will show up in our world?" she asked, quite seriously, wondering if Artur could fall for one of the women, should another turn up.

"Possibly. They came on a ship from the sky, Dracolin said, and Persephonice had told him that there were numerous ships like that all over. That each of them were filled with more of her kind."

"What would you do if you ran into a redheaded woman who looked like a mermaid who could walk on land?" She raised a brow.

"Both of the women had magical abilities. I would rather settle down with a woman—an elf woman—who is normal like me."

Rina laughed. He would not like to hear that she had abilities of her own that would make her far superior to him then. And what did it mean to be normal anyway? She felt she was perfectly normal. But then she wondered—when he had come to her aid before—had he not seen her disappear from the back of a dark arts knight's horse and reappear to cut off the head of another of the enemy knights?

"What about you? If a male from one of those ships came to our world? Could you be swayed to entertain and marry him?" Artur asked.

Smiling, Rina said, "If he had magical abilities, it would

depend on what kind. If he was truly loyal, then maybe. He would have to be a warrior like me. Some of them are not fighters, but collectors of history. One like that would not do for me."

THOUGH MIRABELLA DID NOT WANT Leogane for her husband, she did not want him murdered over her either. But now the voices swirled around in her head.

"She has told them we are here!"

"She is to be one of us!"

"She will be the death of us!"

Desiring with a vengeance to know if Erlig heard the voices, too, she crushed that notion, figuring that no one seemed to hear anything that she did. She thought at first it was that the canyon walls caused the men's voices to echo off them, though there were no echoes, just the singular comments.

Jeremka, Rina, and Artur and other knights watched behind them, while Erlig kept his horse and attention focused on Leogane and the rest of the men.

The king rode into battle, his gleaming sword catching the sun's rays as he held it high, his tall stature and broad shoulders imposing.

"Kill the king and the rest will give her up!"

"No!" she shouted.

"What's the matter, my lady?" Erlig asked.

"They...they want to kill the king."

Erlig smiled. "They are welcome to try."

She held her arms around herself, the chill in the air seeming to intensify.

"Do you hear them speaking still?"

She shook her head, having said too much already.

"Did you smell the boar cooking outside the healer's hut?"

"'Twas a strong scent. Anyone would have smelled it."

"Aye." But the way the king's advisor answered her, she did not think he believed her. "How long have you been able to hear so acutely, my lady?"

She didn't speak for fear of incriminating herself.

"You seem surprised that you have this ability that no one else seems to have. I would venture to say you are gaining some unique abilities as you grow older. Can you do magic?"

She opened her mouth to argue with him, but just then three men dressed in chain mail and the familiar black tunics emblazoned with a red rose jumped out at the king from behind the colorful clay rocks. Two swung swords at him, but when the rest of the king's escort caught up with them, Vladek's men were easily cut down.

"They thought there were fewer of us left," she said under her breath.

"Us?"

"Of you, the king and your men," she quickly corrected.

"Is that why there were fewer of them this time? They didn't think the king and our men would be so...invincible?"

She thought there was a hint of threat in Erlig's words, but when she studied him, he only smiled back.

For some strange reason, maybe because the king's advisor had a daughter most likely near her age, maybe because he acted as her guard, but was not mean like the ones her uncle posted for her, maybe because he reminded her of her father, she felt the urge to tell this man things she'd allowed to fester deep inside her for too long. Whether he believed her or not, it didn't matter.

"My uncle killed my father," she said, softly. She'd only said the words in anger to her uncle and had been whipped severely by him for the outburst. She'd told others when she was little and was locked up in the Castle Mayden tower for her indiscretions. What would it matter if she told Erlig who would no doubt disbelieve her anyway? At least she would say her mind.

"'Twas a hunting accident, my lady." Though he spoke gently, his gray eyes continued to watch her as if to see her response.

"Aye, a planned and executed, cold-blooded hunting accident. If I hadn't been told so many times by my guardian, Phiri, that I killed my mother in childbirth, I would think my uncle had murdered her too." She looked at Erlig to see his response to that.

His eyes turned hard, as if annoyed she would be so confused about what had happened in the past. That she would condemn her uncle for unspeakable things. "You have it all wrong, my lady. 'Twas a hunting accident, nothing more."

"Why was I locked in the tower then?"

"I assume His Grace did so to protect you."

She gave a short derisive laugh, then listened to Leogane give orders to his men. As before, they examined the bodies, lifting helmets high, where only powdered dust remained, spilling from the iron masks, scattering on the breeze.

"If King Inari had some other reason to keep you at Castle Mayden, pray tell what it was," Erlig said.

She watched as Leogane looked back at her, and seeing she was still with his advisor, he remounted his horse and spoke again to his men. "My uncle could not stand looking at me, seeing the hatred I had for him, knowing I knew he was my father's murderer and stole the crown. I've always thought he was the kind of man who cared not a whit about what any of his people thought of his actions, but it seems when it comes to me, he feels guilty. So during the year after my father's murder, my uncle locked me away at Mayden."

"But you had free rein of the castle and of the servants."

"Of my chamber, you mean. And no, I was in charge of no one."

"He wouldn't have—"

"Have you never seen him beat a man or woman near death before? Or murder someone just because the person disagreed with him. I have. He is a tyrant."

Erlig shifted uneasily in his saddle.

"Come now, you cannot say you have only witnessed my uncle use kindness."

Clearing his throat, Erlig said, "He has always been fair minded and the most gracious of hosts when the king and I have visited."

"Count Vladek, no doubt, will not be misled by my uncle."

Leogane galloped back to them, sweat dribbling from his furrowed brow, his horse kicking up the dust. "We move forward through the pass now, but I want you to ride up ahead with me, Princess Mirabella."

So he believed her now. She wasn't sure if this was a good thing or bad. Pursing her lips, she didn't want the king to use her, then cast her aside when he didn't need her any longer. Then she sighed deeply. She didn't want her escort harmed either. For now, she would aid the king and his men, but later, she would be the sliver in his sword hand that he would soon want to be rid of.

Jeremka brought her horse, and once she had mounted him, she and Leogane moved slowly through the pass, while she listened for any sound, any whispered words. "I hear none but your men speaking about my strange ability and how worried they are that I might attack you when you sleep."

Leogane turned and gave Erlig a look. The wordless communication spurred his advisor to return to the men who followed them some distance behind.

She heard Erlig telling the men to cease their prattle, making her smile, glad that she was not the only one who was told to terminate her words. She glanced at the king who watched her with a mixture of fascination and concern. Then he looked back at his men when Erlig kicked his horse and rejoined them, just slightly behind Mirabella's horse, probably to ensure she was protected in the event she didn't hear anyone ahead, and they were attacked anyway.

Their horses' hooves clip-clopped on the stone floor of the canyon, almost deafening as it echoed off the canyon walls.

Every time they drew close to an outcropping of rocks, they paused and waited for her to tell them if the area was clear. It should have made her proud she could accomplish something no one else could, something worthy of praise. But the men seemed uneasy of her ability which confirmed the healer imposter's words that Mirabella would be better off with her own kind.

By the time they exited the long narrow pass, it stretched so high it was taller than the castle towers at Castle Mayden, blocking out the sun in places. The golden sphere dipped behind the mountains and a sparkling blue lake beckoned to her. Instantly, she remembered how years ago she had picnicked with several maids near a lake such as this. Immediately she drew her horse closer.

"Lake Orcy," Leogane informed her. "'Tis said a giant from beyond the mountains of the Five Sisters of Kintail stomped his foot in anger, attempting to squash an annoying bird and left the crater. He broke his ankle and cried for half a year, filling the hole with his tears."

"'Tis salty then?" she asked.

"Nay. The rains over the centuries have diluted it until it became a freshwater lake." He smiled.

Did he think her foolish for believing the tale?

She jumped down from her horse, crouched at the water's

edge, and stuck her hand in. The water felt warm and silky against her skin. "'Tis warm."

"Aye, they say underwater vents heat the water."

"Can I bathe?"

"Nay."

She frowned at him, feeling filthy from the dirt kicked up by their horses. She imagined her face was covered in dust, and her hair was no longer blond but brown. "But no more of Vladek's men are in the area."

The king raised his dark brows. "But my men are."

"They can turn their backs."

Leogane turned to his advisor. "Have the men prepare camp."

"Aye, my lord." Erlig moved in the direction of the men and gave the orders.

Turning to face her, Leogane said, "If we had a tent, you could bathe, my lady, with my blessing, but not out in the open."

She grabbed a pack off her horse. "You are insufferable. You know that?" The water was too inviting to ignore.

"I was thinking the same of you. It would be nice if for once when I told you to do something, or that you should not do something, you would obey me without argument."

"Would Erlig's daughter be so complacent?"

"I think the term is agreeable. And aye, that she would. The perfect wife."

"Good then. You can leave me here for Vladek and continue home to the one you love." But she didn't mean it. She wanted to go with Rina and find another way to oust her uncle from her father's throne.

Leogane scowled at her, shook his head, and stalked off, giving one last order to Erlig. "Watch her." He glanced at Artur and Rina.

They both inclined their heads and joined the princess and Erlig.

"You would think he doesn't trust me," she said to Erlig while she removed the satin ribbons from her hair.

"What makes you think that, my lady?"

"He always has you guard me."

"He wants no one to seize you and take you away."

She unwound her braids, more of the hair undone than braided. "What about you? Surely you would love to ensure your daughter and not I would wed the king."

"I wish what is best for His Grace. If he decides he wishes you instead of my daughter to be his bride—"

"I want him not," Mirabella snapped back. The king was too loyal to her uncle. No way could she convince him that he had murdered her father.

Folding his arms, Erlig's gray eyes studied her. "Aye, but 'tis not your decision. What do you know of Vladek?"

"Nothing. I've never met him."

"And you want to marry him because?"

"That is an idiotic question. He wants me. Your lord doesn't. Simple as that. And...I don't want him anyway. I want my uncle to pay for his crimes."

"Vladek won't be happy you're warning us about his men."

She sat down on the grass and pulled off her leather shoes and hose, mulling over that notion. "I won't allow him to kill all of you when he has no business doing so."

To Mirabella's surprise, Rina took hold of Justina's arm and forced her to join the princess. "You are the princess's maid. Earn your keep."

Seeing Rina's scowl, the princess turned to Justina and said, "I know you had just arrived at Mayden Castle, and you only know me based on what others have said, but I would like to... have good relations between us."

The maid looked haughtily at her, like the princess was beneath her. Mirabella didn't understand why the woman would treat her like that now that they were no longer at Mayden Castle. If Mirabella did wed Leogane, it would be up to her as to who would be on her staff. So it would behoove Justina to treat her nicely for now!

Rina looked at Justina with an expression that said she'd better change her attitude or else.

Still looking mulish, Justina began to comb out the princess's hair. Rina appeared poised to take the maid to task if she pulled at Mirabella's hair in the least bit harshly.

Mirabella knew the warrior elf was only here to aid her, not be her friend, but she felt as though she was the only one here who truly had her best interests at heart.

10

A fter the princess cleaned up and her hair was once again tidy, Rina and Leogane's party ate broth and bread. Erlig and several knights watched over the king and the princess while Artur and Rina provided guard duty further out with others.

"What do you think about the princess?" Rina asked Artur.

"She is beautiful."

Rina was thinking more in terms of personality. She ate some of her broth and shook her head.

"She is."

"I agree. I was thinking about her willfulness."

"All right. She has determination, so I think she will try to make trouble for her uncle. If King Leogane doesn't believe her story that her uncle had her father killed, she will make trouble for him as well."

Rina nodded. She'd thought the same thing.

"She is stubborn. And that could be a hassle for my king. Truly willful." Artur ate some more of his bread.

"What of the king's interest in his advisor's daughter?" Rina would want her husband to love her, no other. She was but a warrior, not a royal pawn. Sometimes royalty married for love, sometimes for other reasons. Rina thought she would marry for love, but what if she found a powerful warrior who was even more well off than she was? Nah, she wanted to marry for love.

Artur thought about it for a while, then he said, "Lady Callie was the king's only choice before the princess's uncle offered her as a bride choice. Leogane did not expect the news and so he was not really all that interested."

"In the princess? But not in Erlig's daughter either?"

Artur glanced around at the other knights who were guarding the camp, and she suspected she was about to hear some juicy court gossip. Normally, she really wasn't into stuff like that. But if it meant the princess would be better off not staying with Leogane, she wanted to hear of it.

She waited. Artur seemed reluctant to say anything. She could understand that. Just because he undoubtedly heard court gossip, it didn't mean he would willingly pass it along to just anyone. Especially someone he didn't know well at all. And maybe not even to his friends. She heard gossip all the time and she rarely shared it with anyone unless it had to do with someone being hurt or killed and then she had to learn if the gossip was true.

"So the king is not all that interested in marrying either of the women," Rina said, then ate another bite of her bread.

"I did not say that."

"No, I just made the conjecture up off the top of my head, based on observations, of course." Rina sat back against the trunk of a tree. "Maybe someone like me would be a good choice of bride for the king."

That got a laugh out of Artur.

She smiled. She loved his laughter. "I'm serious." She paused and thought about her attributes that the king might like. "I'm quiet."

Artur raised his brows, a hint of a smile on his lips.

"When I need to be. I often am on my own when I'm on my missions and so unless I begin talking to myself, I'm very quiet."

"Do you talk to yourself very often?"

"Sometimes. When I have no impending threat and I'm voicing something I've been mulling over out loud. Haven't you?"

He shook his head.

"That you won't admit to! I'm good with people and would be fair to servants."

Again, Artur's brows rose.

Recalling that she had forcibly made Justina help the princess with her hair at the lake, Rina let her breath out in exasperation. "The princess hasn't ever been in charge of her staff. Her uncle was, from everything I've overheard her say. She wants to make friends with Justina because she has had no friends since she was locked in the tower. Maybe not even before that. Justina wouldn't move a step in the princess's direction to help her with her hair. I didn't have the authority to command the girl to do her duty, but I wasn't about to let her get away with doing naught at all. So I did what I would normally do in a situation like that. I took charge."

"Bodily."

"Aye." Let Artur stew on that for a while. Rina wouldn't have done anything differently. She didn't care if he didn't approve of her actions or not.

"The princess should have dealt with her." Artur picked up a stick and doodled on the ground.

"Aye."

He drew a crescent moon. "You interceded and didn't give her the opportunity to straighten Justina out herself."

"Did you notice that your king was watching the situation also? That he didn't approve of Justina's attitude? That he was waiting for someone else to take charge and force the maid to do her job? So don't you see? Mayhap the king will believe I can take charge of the staff and get them to do their work when they balk at it."

Artur chuckled.

"Given time, I work well with others. This is an extraordinary case. Most of the time, servants are happy to work for their masters, if they are paid well and treated with respect. In this situation, it's like the princess's uncle told his staff to be mean to the princess no matter what it took. So Justina is a product of that. She doesn't have that older woman to tell her what to do either. Justina is not the usual servant on a royal staff."

"True."

"Lastly, I could protect the king even in his bedchamber at night." Rina smiled at Artur.

"Wouldn't you tire of wearing frilly gowns, like the princess will wear? Wouldn't you miss fighting battles, solving cases, defending the weak and innocent? I would think that attendance at fine balls and other necessary social functions would not appeal to you."

"Maybe they would, if I had the king to dance with."

Artur looked out at the woods, listening for any other sounds other than the breeze blowing the tree branches, the green leaves fluttering in the wind. "I think they have left us alone for the moment."

"Don't jinx us," she said.

Artur stared at her in surprise. "You are superstitious?"

"Isn't everybody?"

"No."

"I've been thinking that Vladek, or someone who works for him, is a dark arts druid. I've killed one before. They're not impossible to eliminate, but they—"

Artur was gaping at her.

She frowned at him. "You don't believe I have."

"I've never heard of one. Come, we must speak with the king. He will want to know this." Artur rose to his feet and offered his hand to her, but she jumped up on her own.

She was not a princess who needed coddling.

"You know, I would offer my hand in help to any knight friend to pull them up." Artur sounded annoyed with her.

"I would not."

"You're a woman. You should not."

She glowered at him. Those were fighting words. He smiled at her as if he knew he'd riled her with his comment.

When they reached the king, he was standing, getting ready to leave. He helped the princess to stand, which was the right thing to do in *her* case!

"Rina needs to speak to you about her concern," Artur said to the king.

"Aye?" the king said, frowning.

"The knights we've been fighting are just like the dark arts knights I've fought before in a different place. They were wearing different tunics with a different emblem, but as with these, they disintegrate into dust when dead. That's how I knew to kill their kind. I've had to before."

"Tell him the rest," Artur said, sounding like they all knew that part, but not the rest.

"A dark arts druid was creating them from black magic. I had to kill him too. It was not easy." She still didn't want to reveal her ability to cloak herself to the king and his men. Some things were better left unsaid. But she knew he'd want to know how he and his men could defeat such a creature. She sighed. "All right. I can...hide myself with a unique ability I have. It was the only way I could get close enough to behead him. I don't know if a blade to the heart would do the trick, but decapitation works.

He was flesh and blood and did not turn to dust like the ones he had created. I believe that either Vladek is a dark arts druid, or he has one working for him. To end the reign of terror he's bringing down on us, we have to kill the druid, whoever he is."

"What about his dark arts knights then? Do they perish along with him? Or will they still fight us?" Artur asked before the king could.

"They will still fight us. They were given orders to do so and will until the last one is standing. But at least once the druid is dead, no more will be created."

"Was the druid working for someone else?" the king asked.

"No. That time he wanted to overtake a princedom in the north. I wasn't there because of him. I was there to find a missing girl. They had laid siege to the walled city and would kill anyone who might try to reach it. It just so happened the girl I was looking for was missing from the princedom when I ran into these dark arts knights. Because of my special abilities, I was able to slip past them, get into the city, learn that the prince and his people were unable to fight the scourge, and so I had to learn what I could do to get the upper hand in this. Once I left the walled city and finally learned how to kill the dark arts knights, I had to return to the castle to let the prince know how his warriors could deal with them. That's when I saw the druid in the woods outside the walls right before my eyes. He didn't see me as I blended in with one of the trees. I couldn't believe a druid would be involved in this."

"Then you killed him," Artur said, sounding amazed that she could do such a thing.

"Not right away. I was too far away from him. My clothes and weapons blend in with the objects I want to hide next to. If I'd had a crossbow with me, I could have shot a bolt into his dark heart from a distance. But at the time, I wasn't even sure that would work on one of his kind. So if I had tried and failed, he would have known I could lurk nearby like that and I would have been killed for certain. Instead, I knew I had to get close enough to him to lop off his head. I figured there would be no way that he could survive that. But I also assumed I would have only one chance at doing it so I had to make it count."

She realized then everyone was listening to her, still watching the woods for any threat, but eager to hear her story. She let out her breath. "The druid seemed to never sleep. I watched him for hours. I was tired at that point. I even fell asleep myself for a while, though when I jerked awake, it nearly gave me a heart attack. I didn't know if I could fall sleep like that and still maintain my chameleon-like form. I've never had to do that before. The thing of it was the woods were filled with those creatures, so any one of them could have discovered me at any time. The creatures he conjured up didn't eat. But the druid did. So while he was cooking a boar on a spit, I moved from tree to tree, getting closer to him. The knights were milling about, just awaiting his orders. I was tired, weary of waiting, hungry too. The smell of the boar made me want to snatch a piece and eat it."

Artur smiled.

"The druid was leaning over, adding another piece of wood to the fire. There were no trees close to him. I did the only thing I could think of doing and it wasn't a good plan at all. I laid on the ground, then inched my way toward him, watching to see that no knights were observing him or looking in my direction. If I stay close to something, like a wall, I can move along its whole length without being seen."

"You were in the great hall during the meal!" the princess exclaimed, looking awed.

"I was. I wanted to know what King Leogane was like. I had to know if he was worthy of your hand in marriage, or if you were even agreeable to the notion."

Artur glanced at the king to see his response. Leogane was just raptly listening to Rina's story, probably trying to recall if he had seen anything amiss in the great hall like Artur was trying to remember.

"But moving from one tree to another means that while I traversed the distance between the trees, I was out in the open and visible. So I wasn't sure how well I could camouflage myself while crawling along the ground. I also didn't know what powers the druid had. Like yours, princess, with the ability to hear sounds and smell scents so much greater than the average elf, if he'd had those, he might have realized I was moving toward him. I also had the problem that I could not kill the druid from a prone position in the dirt and grass. I would have to rise up quickly and swing my sword. If I didn't do it while he had his back turned to me, I feared I wouldn't be successful. It might not seem chivalrous, but killing a dark arts druid isn't easy—I didn't figure. I was only one warrior. I knew his knights would swarm me too once they saw what I was about to do, if they noticed. So I didn't really have any choice."

"So you rose up, swung your sword, and cut off his head," Artur said, sounding impatient for her to finish the rest of the story.

"I rose up, he turned, I about had a heart attack, I think he did too, his mouth agape and eyes were huge. I swung my sword and decapitated him. His head rolled into the fire, cooking below the boar. I wanted so badly to slice off a piece of the cooked boar, but his knights shouted, and I ran for the nearest horse that I could find, jumped into the saddle, and rode out of their camp. I could hear a whole cavalcade of horses gathering to chase me down. But all I needed to do was lean into the horse, blend with it, confusing the ones who had taken chase. It appeared then that the riderless horse was on its own and they turned back to search the woods for where I'd fallen off. I rode the horse all the way to the city wall, leapt off, and made my way to the place on the wall where I'd climbed it before. Once I was inside the city walls, I had another audience with the prince, told him what had happened, and he sent out his soldiers to fight the dark arts knights until they were vanquished. I helped them, of course. I had to make sure they killed every one of them for good. Then I searched for the missing girl and found her hiding in a cave nearby. She told me she had seen the dark arts knights while she was picking flowers in the meadow and couldn't return to her home. So all ended well."

Everyone was quiet for a while, then the king said, "I'm glad you are on our side then. How do we find this druid?"

"He will be in the center of his encampment. He doesn't need to watch the men he sends to kill us. He will stay back to keep from getting into a skirmish himself. He might be a powerful druid, capable of creating these undead creatures—at least that's what I figure they are—but when it comes to his own physical body, a druid is not all powerful. At least that's the way it seemed to me with the last one I had to kill. Either Vladek is the druid and then we need to locate him and kill him, or he has someone working for him who is. In which case, we will need to eliminate both of them because I doubt Vladek will give up on trying to take the princess for his own even if he loses his druid."

11

Artur was shocked that Rina had been able to take down a powerful druid and knew he should have kept his mouth shut when she was trying to tell her story. But he oft looked at the last pages in a book he was reading to learn how the story ended, so he couldn't help himself when he blurted out the words. He swore Erlig shook his head at him, but he was wearing a smile when he had. Artur had probably annoyed Rina, but he was much impressed that she didn't freeze when the druid turned to face her, and she swung her sword and killed him.

He wondered then what other feats she had accomplished. He knew Dracolin was famous for his, but Artur had never heard of Rina before.

The king asked Erlig, Artur, and Rina to join him to have a talk. Artur wouldn't have expected him to ask Rina to meet with him to decide on their next plan of action, until she had revealed what they were probably up against and how she had defeated a druid like the one they most likely needed to eliminate.

"Since you have done this before, Rina, what do you recommend?" the king asked her.

She took a deep breath. "I need to go into the woods. I can protect the princess with the party, but I need to scout out where Vladek or his druid, if he is not one, is."

"I will go with her," the princess said, joining them in the discussion though she had not been invited.

"Not on my life," the king said, looking sternly at her.

"Rina is right. I can hear and smell things better than the rest of you can. Not only that, but I hear their voices in my head," Mirabella said.

"Whose?" the king asked.

"The ones who are trying to kill you. Vladek's. His men speak and I hear them," the princess said.

"Can you hear what we are thinking?" Artur asked.

"No, not thinking. I...I believe they can communicate without speaking out loud like we do," the princess said.

"I'm going with you, Rina," Artur said.

"No way. I have to do this alone." Rina motioned to his armor. "You are too shiny, too noisy."

He began stripping off his armor. Her mouth gaped. Artur wasn't letting her go into the woods alone. Not only because he wanted to help her, but he wanted to make sure she was telling the truth. He believed she was, but if there was a glimmer of a chance she wasn't, he had to know that too. What if she was who she told them she was and she found Vladek, but she didn't make it out of there alive? At least one of them had to get back to the king and report.

"You cannot blend with the trees or other objects. You won't last a minute in the woods on your own with the knights all about. When his dark arts knights see you, I will have to attempt to save you. Then the knights would know I'm cloaking myself. We would both be at risk."

"I'm going with you. I'll stay away from you. Without my armor, I can move just as quietly as you. I might not be able to cloak myself like you can, but I am trained to move silently in the woods as a warrior elf would also. I can stay away from you so that I don't bring the enemy down on you. Don't reveal yourself if I get myself into trouble."

"Ha, as if I'd let that happen."

"I'm not going to let you go by yourself."

"The king and the princess need you to be here for them," Rina said.

Artur wasn't sure how the king would feel about it. Leogane actually agreed with Artur. "He will go with you."

RINA COULDN'T BELIEVE it when the king said Artur would go with her. That was such a messed-up plan. Of course if the dark arts knights realized Artur was in their midst, she would come to his aid. He couldn't have been serious when he told her to remain cloaked. She wasn't a warrior for nothing. But she did love her own way of doing things and this wasn't her way.

"All right. But don't say I didn't tell you so." At least underneath the armor, he was wearing padded leather armor, more similar to what she wore. "And if you get me killed, I will never forgive you." Not to mention she wouldn't forgive herself if she wasn't able to save him either. "Got your sword? Water flask? Something to eat, if this takes us a while?"

"Aye. I'm ready."

"Let's go." Rina prayed they wouldn't run into real trouble, that they would learn what they needed to, and a real bonus? If they could discover the druid causing all the problems, and better yet, kill him.

The princess still looked like she wanted to go with them because they could use her abilities. Rina said to her, "If you were in the middle of their kind, they'd grab you. They might even be able to sense it. We just can't risk you being in the middle of danger. I don't think they'd hurt you, but once they had you, you'd have no choice. You'd be stuck with them. King Leogane could try and rescue you, of course, but what if you'd changed your mind?"

The princess didn't say anything.

"Okay, we're going," Rina said, and she and Artur went on foot into the woods.

They were both quiet, moving together but apart just like they needed to do. She was glad. She didn't want to be on top of him if they ran across the knights. That way whoever had the confrontation first, the other could be there as backup.

She continued to move quietly through the woods, figuring the knights wouldn't be that far from Leogane's party, watching them silently in the dark.

"THE PRINCESS BELIEVES, my lord, that her uncle murdered her father," Erlig told the king privately.

"Why?"

"I didn't ask. I believe she was hurt by her father's death and blames her uncle. Another matter, though. We know now she seems to hear what the rest of us cannot," Erlig said.

"Aye."

"I was close enough to you when you spoke to the maid about the princess, and though she was in the healer's hut at the time..."

Leogane glanced at Mirabella, her eyes shut tight, her breathing shallow in sleep as they waited for word from Rina and Artur about Vladek or a druid menace. "You think she might have overheard what the maid said?"

"I think it's a possibility. I've never met anyone who could hear like she does. Only the animals can hear like that. You asked me earlier if I could smell the meat cooking when I was in the hut with the imposter. Why did you ask this of me, my lord?"

"She said the meat was not done cooking. I knew she spoke the truth, but could not understand how she would know. She had not seen us spit the meat. She wouldn't have known how long it was hanging above the flames."

"She assumed it hadn't been long enough?"

Shaking his head, Leogane glanced back at the fire. "Nay, I don't think so. If she's been locked in the tower for years, she would have no idea how long it takes to cook meat over an open fire."

"So you're saying?"

The king straightened his back and looked at the figure half buried in blankets. "Her sense of smell is truly more acute as well." He glanced at Justina, sleeping near the princess.

"Do you think it was a good idea sending Artur with Rina to search for Vladek and the druid?" Erlig asked.

"I felt I didn't have any choice. He has a good head on his shoulders. He knows how to move in the woods like a warrior elf and fight well. If Rina needs his help, he'll be there for her, and the same for him, if he needs her help."

"But you also want to have him spy on her to ensure she's not in the enemy's camp?" Erlig asked.

Leogane smiled. "I doubt she is because she has been killing the dark arts knights every bit as much as we have. But it would be good to have Artur there too."

THE PRINCESS WAS PERTURBED that she wasn't able to go with Rina and Artur on their search for the druid. She really felt she might have aided them with her ability to hear so well. She was astonished that Rina had such an amazing cloaking ability. Then she wondered if that's why she couldn't see Rina when she looked out the tower window. She appeared to have vanished and she had—through her cloaking ability.

Mirabella had heard the king talking to his advisor about her. He didn't seem to have as much animosity for Mirabella now and she was feeling better about that. If he would only believe her about what her uncle had done and help her take action against him, she could be allied with the king, and he could then marry his advisor's daughter. She just had to convince him of it.

She rolled over on the bedding and saw the king watching her. Erlig had taken off to talk to some of their men and she decided to make her proposal to Leogane. "You know my uncle had my father killed to take the crown."

"So I've heard. You were there and saw it?" Leogane asked.

"I was. I was determined to go with my father on the hunt. I saw my uncle direct one of his men to shoot my father. My father died instantly, and my uncle immediately returned to the castle to take over the kingdom. He left my father's body in the woods, and I...I tried to wake him, but he was truly dead. Then I heard someone coming. A woodcutter with a cart. I hid in the woods and watched as he took my father's body back to the castle for burial."

"Do you have any proof?"

"I have the signet ring my father wore. I took it from him, the only thing I'd have to remember him by when I heard the cart coming and then hid. I heard my uncle ask the woodcutter later where my father's ring was. When the woodcutter told him he hadn't seen it, my uncle was furious and knew the woodcutter had stolen the ring. He had him beaten, trying to learn where he'd put the ring. When the woodcutter wouldn't tell him, my uncle had him killed. The woodcutter's name was Elijah. He had a family—a wife and two children he'd left behind. His wife, Agnes, would know about her husband's death and the reason for it."

"You have the ring?"

"Aye. I kept it hidden always." She pulled the necklace off her neck and showed the ring to him. "If my uncle had learned I had the ring, he most likely would have assumed I had taken it from my father. That I had witnessed his murder. I don't believe he would have thought the woodsman would have given it to me and then refused to tell him I had it, knowing my uncle would have him killed. Everyone knows what he is like. My father had kept his younger brother in check before that, but now that Inari has free reign over our people, there's no stopping him."

Leogane just studied the signet ring.

"I have a proposal to make to you."

Leogane's gaze shot up to hers and she figured women didn't ever make proposals to him, but at least he was still listening.

"If you help me to remove my uncle as king and I take over, I will form an alliance with you. Then you can marry your advisor's daughter." Mirabella thought everything she said sounded completely reasonable. Unless the king still didn't believe her, or he figured he could make an alliance with her uncle without having to lose his men in battle if he just wed Mirabella.

"You are different than I thought you were."

"I was imprisoned in the tower. You are here because you are working with my uncle. How do you think I felt about that?"

"It's understandable how you feel. I'll give your proposal consideration."

He was the king. He made all the decisions. He could just tell her he was going to help her! She should have known he wouldn't.

12

Artur was keeping up with Rina, looking for any sign of the dark arts knights when he saw one of them lurking in the woods. He didn't see his horse. In the other encounters, the men all rode horses. If Artur eliminated him, would others be nearby and hear them fighting? Warning them that their enemy was coming for them?

But he didn't want to run into this one if he ended up in a fight with another. He moved quietly toward the dark arts knight when he suddenly saw Rina materialize and behead the knight. He moved quickly to her location and helped her to hide the knight's armor since the rest of him had turned to dust. Artur didn't want anyone to find the armor and sound the alarm.

"There are three more over there," Rina said, whispering in Artur's ear. Her soft breath tickled his ear and for an insane minute, he wanted to turn and kiss her. She frowned at him. "Pay attention."

He nodded. "We take care of them."

"Right. I haven't seen any sign of the enemy's camp," she said, her voice just as hushed. "I'll take the two on the right, you get the one on the left."

"Aye." If Artur had been all macho, he might have felt offended, but he wasn't because he assumed she'd do a better job at taking two of them down because of her ability to hide from them.

They started to move toward the knights when Rina did her disappearing act, but nearly as soon as she did, she grabbed his arm and nearly made his heart quit beating. "What?" he whispered. They had a plan.

"There's a whole encampment that way. Do you smell the smoke? Do you see little bit of lights through the trees over there? We need to move that way and see if we can get closer to the campfire. We need to learn if someone in charge of the dark arts knights is over there."

"Okay, let's do it."

"Carefully," she said.

"Of course." She didn't need to tell Artur that. He carefully moved toward the encampment, losing sight of Rina right away.

He moved as close to the campfire as he could. Standing around the campfire were three men who were not wearing helmets and armor—the one whom he recognized—Vladek. Gods, if Artur had had his crossbow, he could kill him right here and now. But two other men were there also, and he wondered if they were his advisors, or even possibly druids? A few others were getting ready to bed down for the night. They appeared to be elven knights—none of them wearing their armor at the moment.

He hoped Rina didn't try and get close to them to kill Vladek or either of the other men. She couldn't take them all out. She couldn't even get close enough to one of them since there was nothing she could camouflage herself with that was that close to the three men, which reminded Artur of the story she had told them about crawling across the ground to reach the druid. But she couldn't do that here. Not with three of them there.

Artur moved nearer to the encampment and heard Vladek speaking to the other two men. "I will have her."

"Your men aren't able to take Leogane's knights down," one of the other men said.

"That's your fault, isn't it, Cabrillo?" Vladek asked. "And yours, Lentil."

The man named Lentil was black haired and bearded, looking into the fire, not speaking to Vladek, as if he was mesmerized by the flames.

"You said you only needed strong, armored knights who could ride well," Cabrillo said.

"Who could *kill*."

"They can fight," Cabrillo said. "They are good at fighting."

"But they are not killing Leogane's men!" Vladek sounded like he could kill *Cabrillo* himself.

Artur wished he would. Then there'd be one less to worry about.

"There is a way," Lentil said, stroking his long beard.

"Well?" Vladek sounded furious he didn't just tell him without prompting him to.

Artur suspected the way in which the druid could make the knights fight better came at a price and that's why they hadn't already empowered them even more.

"They will be fiercer, more determined, more deadly," Lentil said.

"Then do it!" Vladek said.

"But we will have much less control over them," Cabrillo quickly said. "We can control them now, direct them where to go, but anyone in Leogane's party would be at risk, including the princess."

Vladek paced next to the fire. "The witch was supposed to bring the princess to me."

"She didn't hide the healer's body well enough. They found

it too quickly," Lentil said. "Rumors are circulating that the princess has been revealing some of our archers' positions."

"She wouldn't know that unless...she's coming into some of her abilities," Vladek said. "I've communicated with her, but she doesn't respond so I believed she didn't have her abilities yet. I should have reached Castle Mayden before Leogane did."

"You didn't find out until it was too late that he was going to see her. Even then, you weren't sure he was going to like her well enough to take her with him. There is another woman that he wishes to marry," Lentil said. "Her guardian was supposed to help us get the princess. Her maid even. But Leogane didn't take her guardian with them and the maid accompanying the princess is way too much of a mouse."

"So what do you want to do?" Cabrillo said.

"I want the princess separated from her escort and then you can make our knights stronger, capable of actually killing Leogane and his men," Vladek growled.

"We can't get close enough to the king and his men to grab her," Lentil said.

Vladek ran his hands through his hair. "You have to. Do whatever it takes."

Suddenly, a hand was on Artur's arm, and he thought a dark arts knight had found him, though if one had, Artur would have been dead. He turned to see Rina and took a relieved breath.

"Come, we need to return to our camp," Rina whispered to him.

"Aye." Then the two of them began to make their trek back to the trail where the king and his party were waiting.

But this time, they ran into trouble. They were in between the dark arts knights and Vladek's encampment, a small area free of any of the enemy's forces, and then more of them. Artur paused, seeing five knights spread out ahead of him.

He tried to go around them but there were more of them.

Still, there was an area where they weren't massed, and he was trying to move through the "safety zone" without being seen. He was glad that at least Rina was more hidden from view.

He realized in that moment how he'd said he wouldn't be interested in a woman who had magical abilities. He was quickly changing his mind about that. She could be invaluable to a fighting force. He couldn't believe she would think the king would want to wed her. Though Artur figured she'd even said so to annoy him. Which he had to admit she had done to an extent. And being interested in some langolar from some other world? He wanted to scoff at that, until Rina pinched his arm.

"Pay attention. Move."

He nearly smiled, but the situation was far too dangerous for that.

It wasn't too much longer after that, that he couldn't slip by a knight and quickly engaged him. Unfortunately, there were more of them that converged on him. Thankfully, Rina was with him, hidden, then out of hiding and attacking the knights as fast as he was.

She blended against a tree and then he struck a knight, and she reappeared, hitting the knight at the same time. He wanted to tell her to get her own targets and not waste her energy on taking down the same knight. Not when they suddenly had a swarm of several of the dark knights upon them.

They had killed about six of them and he was glad that the druid hadn't made them any stronger or more vicious or he and Rina wouldn't have managed to annihilate them.

Rina grabbed Artur's hand as he cut off the head of another knight and ran to a massive oak tree. As soon as they made it to the tree, she wrapped her arms around Artur and leaned him against the tree. What...?

The knights were swarming all around them and they didn't seem to notice them. Artur couldn't believe it and he kept expecting the knights to see them. They were brushing past them, so close he felt the breeze stirred up by their movement. Rina's body was pressed against him as tight as she could, and her head was resting against his chest. If any of the knights saw him, he wouldn't be able to swing his sword to defend her.

But she wasn't moving while the knights were frantically looking for them.

It seemed like forever before the knights began to disperse. She whispered to him, "Are you ready to move again?"

He kind of liked this time alone with her, but he knew they needed to get out of here and get the word to the king about what was going on. Not to mention they couldn't hold this position forever.

"Yeah. Let's go." Things had really quieted down and the knights weren't close to them now, still searching for them but closer to where Artur and Rina had killed the others of their kind.

They quietly moved away from the knights, trying to reach the trail without engaging any more of the dark arts knights. But then they came across another group of them, seven in number, watching the king's encampment. They tried to skirt around them, but that was taking them farther away from the king's party. Once they reached the trail, they would be on their own, exposed to any knights that might be watching it. Though they probably would be observing the king's party from the woods, and not searching for stragglers.

Rina suddenly whistled and Artur wondered what she was doing. Then he heard a horse coming. At first, he thought it was a dark arts knight riding a horse, but then he saw it was Rina's horse. As soon as her horse was close enough, she jumped on his back and offered her hand to Artur. He took her hand and slid behind her. Two of them on her horse would slow them down and they couldn't easily fight on horseback against their enemies like this either.

She kicked her horse on and he took off like the wind. He was beautiful but in motion, truly amazing. They finally reached the trail, and the dark arts knights heard them galloping off.

Rina and Artur and her horse kept going, keeping out of the knights' reach. Then they finally heard someone on the trail ahead of them and he hoped it was his men, not the enemy.

But there were four dark arts knights ready to fight them on the trail ahead.

She was riding toward them. Artur was thinking she should let him off so she could hide herself on her horse's back and he would fight them on foot. But she wasn't slowing down. They waited for them and when they were upon them, she switched her sword to her left hand, surprising him. He swung at the knight to their right while she swung at the one to their left. The other two were closing in when bolts flew toward the last two knights, striking their targets, and the dark arts knights fell off their mounts—dead.

"Stop here," Artur said, seeing some of King Leogane's men riding toward them to offer their support.

"Why?" Rina asked.

"I'll get one of the dead knight's horses."

She pulled her horse to a stop, and Artur jumped off and grabbed one of the knight's horses that was milling around. He leapt into the saddle and headed out with Rina.

"You didn't tell me you are ambidextrous," Artur said.

She laughed. "I don't tell anyone in case I need to swordfight with my left hand and catch them off-guard."

"You are very clever."

"Thank you."

~

RINA COULDN'T BELIEVE she could actually cloak another person with her abilities, but she'd had to do it. When they had been surrounded by the dark knights, they wouldn't have survived if it hadn't been for her abilities. She was amused he was so shocked when she could fight with her left hand just as well as with her right. And she was really glad he had come with her. She thought she'd have done fine on her own, but she had welcomed being with him on this mission, which was really unusual for her.

She was disappointed to learn Vladek had two druids working for him. Who knew if he himself had dark arts abilities.

Then they reached the encampment and met up with the king and Erlig. The princess was sound asleep.

They explained everything they'd learned to the king.

"So taking the druids and Vladek out isn't going to be easy," the king said.

"The problem is that they want to make these creatures even stronger. We're beating them too easily," Rina said.

"But they have to get to the princess first and take off with her or these knights could end up killing her too," Artur said.

"What do you suggest we do?" King Leogane asked.

"As long as we have the princess with us, I don't believe the druids will make their knights any stronger," Rina said. "I suggest we continue on our way to your castle."

"All right. We'll leave at dawn," the king said. "The two of you get some rest."

Gladly. Rina was tired and when she laid out her bedroll, Artur laid his next to hers. "Are you lonely?" she asked him as she laid down and covered herself with a blanket.

Artur scoffed. "If we are attacked in the middle of the night, I want your protection."

She smiled and closed her eyes.

"Thanks for saving our lives back there."

"It was all in a night's work." And then she fell asleep until she smelled porridge and saw the sun peeking through the trees. She groaned. She hadn't had enough sleep. As soon as she rolled up her bedroll, she saw the princess watching her. "Did you have a good sleep, my lady?"

"Aye, once I made my proposal to the king."

Astonished, Rina said, "To marry him?"

"Nay. To be his ally once he ousts my uncle from the castle."

"Oh. And the king agreed?" Rina was a little surprised to hear it.

"He is considering my proposition."

Artur was already up and about and brought them both porridge. He looked ready for the journey again.

"I worried you would not return to us," Mirabella said to Artur.

"Rina kept us safe." Artur took off to speak to his men.

"That takes a good man to admit that a woman could protect him in battle, I'm sure," the princess said to Rina.

"He fought just as hard to keep us safe, but he doesn't feel the need to mention his heroics." Rina ate some more of her porridge. She wanted to ask Mirabella what she would do if the king said he wanted to marry her to obtain an alliance with King Inari. It would be so much easier then going to war with him to put Mirabella on the throne. Though he wouldn't just have an alliance with her, if he also married her. He would have any expanded kingdom.

When they were on the trail traveling again, Rina and Artur stayed near the princess this time.

They fought two more ambushes, both times Mirabella alerting them of the battles ahead of time, giving the king and his men the advantage.

They were finally within a day's ride of Grande Castle and everyone's spirits were lifted.

To Rina's surprise she saw her cousin Dracolin, his dark brown hair and Persephonice's red hair whipping about as they rode a green-scaled dragon, flying toward them. Why? Had they come to see Artur for some reason? Rina knew they wouldn't be looking for her.

13

W hen Artur saw the dragon coming toward them and could recognize Dracolin and Persephonice were riding him, he assumed they were coming to see Rina, but she looked surprised. But Dracolin was her cousin. He wouldn't be coming to see Artur for any reason.

Then the king stopped his party and the dragon landed in the middle of them.

Dracolin jumped off the dragon's back and offered his hand to Persephonice to help her down. Artur glanced at Rina to see if she realized a male warrior could help a female warrior dismount and for it to be perfectly all right.

Rina looked at Artur and smiled.

The king greeted them as if they were royalty.

But then Dracolin saw Rina and said, "We've come for her."

"Rina?" the king asked.

"Aye, her parents said she should never have been this far from home," Dracolin said, looking sternly at her.

Artur glanced at her, waiting for her to say she hadn't gone against their wishes.

"The king has hired me to help him take the princess to his

castle." Rina sounded irritated that her parents would treat her like a kid instead of a warrior, particularly since she'd killed dark arts knights and a druid on her own.

"Aye," King Leogane said, confirming he had hired her.

Frowning, Rina looked annoyed that her family would make a fuss about this. "I'm staying here to help protect Princess Mirabella. We've been besieged several times by dark arts knights." She told Dracolin and Persephonice about Vladek, the druids, and the dark arts knights.

"Wait, like the druids and the other dark arts knights you've killed already?" Dracolin asked.

"Aye," Rina said.

"Rina has been invaluable to us in helping to take down these knights," Artur said to Dracolin. "We were unable to get close enough to eliminate Vladek or the druids, however."

"Good to see you again, Artur," Dracolin said, shaking his hand.

"Same here."

Persephonice walked over and gave Rina a hug. "I'm glad you're fine and that you're helping out here."

"Did my parents really send you to find me?" Rina was still frowning, looking like she could not believe they would embarrass her so.

"Yes. You've been gone for far too long. They said you normally only take jobs closer to home," Dracolin said.

"Ugh," Rina said. "I'd heard the rumors about a princess locked in a tower and I had to investigate to learn the truth."

"In the Black Hills? A Black Hills elf?" Dracolin said, glancing at Mirabella, as if he thought Rina should never have gone that far from the shadow elf kingdom.

"Of course," Rina said. "When we believe a wrong needs to be righted, we have to do it."

"Aye, but you should have told your parents." Dracolin sounded so stern, like he was her older brother.

And Rina was bristling about it. Artur didn't blame her. She was a warrior, and she was really good at it, though she should have probably told her parents where she was going.

Rina scoffed. "Everyone was on a mission when I left to check this out."

"And you didn't leave a note behind," Dracolin said.

"None of us do. We just go."

"But not for that—"

Suddenly they were being attacked again and Dracolin grabbed Mirabella and put her on the back of the dragon. Persephonice leapt onto the dragon, but Dracolin stayed with the party.

"No!" Rina said, shouting at him.

"I'll take the princess to King Leogane's castle. Vladek's men won't be able to get to her," Persephonice said.

"He'll make the dark arts—forget it. Take her safely away from here," Rina said.

Artur understood Rina's concern, but he also knew the princess could be protected in this way and the rest of the warriors would fight the dark arts knights, no matter how powerful they made them. Having Dracolin with them would be good too.

"What about the other woman?" Persephonice asked.

"No," Rina said, already rushing forth to kill a knight.

Persephonice took off before a swarm of dark arts knights attacked the dragon.

Artur believed Rina was right. He didn't trust Justina with the princess. But then he was fighting beside Dracolin and Rina against the knights. They weren't more powerful, but he was afraid Rina was right. Once the word got back to Vladek and the druids, the new knights they had to face would probably be tougher to beat.

He was relieved that the princess was taking off to the king's castle. He swung his sword at another knight and noticed Rina had vanished. He glanced at the ground, worried she might be wounded and on the ground, but she was...gone. He wished he had that talent.

Everyone but the maid was fighting the knights. Then Artur saw the last dark arts knight fall from his horse in the woods. Rina came walking out afterward, sheathing her sword.

Artur couldn't help but admire her for what she could do and swore she did it to prove to Dracolin that she was perfectly capable of dealing with this on her own.

Dracolin looked at her and then at Artur, and Artur figured her cousin wondered if he knew what had happened, if he knew about her ability.

"They know," Rina told Dracolin.

Artur figured she didn't tell everyone about her uniqueness then.

Dracolin got one of the dark arts knight's horses and mounted it. "If you're ready to continue traveling?"

Artur was amused. Dracolin often took charge of a situation, even if he wasn't supposed to be the one who did.

Everyone moved then, doubling up on the trail. Dracolin rode beside Rina, who gave him an annoyed look as he forced Artur to drop back with Jeremka. Erlig was riding beside the king.

Artur missed having the princess's ability to warn them of danger. But he also missed being able to ride beside Rina.

∼

MIRABELLA COULDN'T BELIEVE she'd be riding on a dragon with a woman who wasn't an elf but married to Dracolin when they arrived at the beautiful castle and grounds. Mirabella was relieved to be out of all the conflict and safely within the walls of the castle. But she was disappointed she couldn't continue to give the king and his knights fair warning about impending battles. From what Rina and Artur had told them, the knights Vladek sent would be even more powerful now. She paced across the courtyard when a few people came out to greet her.

"I'm Callie, the king's advisor's daughter, and I want to welcome you to Castle Grande," a pretty dark-haired woman said.

Now this was totally awkward, Mirabella thought.

"Come with me and I'll show you to your quarters." Callie glanced at the dragon in the courtyard and Persephonice. "You too."

"I'm returning to Dracolin and the king. We'll see you later," Persephonice said.

"Be careful," Mirabella told her. "And thank you for bringing me here."

"It's my pleasure. We'll see you soon." Then Persephonice climbed onto the dragon and flew off.

"You and the king were planning to marry?" Mirabella asked, as Callie escorted her into the castle with two other ladies-in-waiting.

"Uh, well, if there hadn't been anyone else, but"—Callie smiled broadly—"I'm so excited to meet you."

Mirabella explained about her uncle.

"Oh." Callie looked horror stricken. But before she could say anything further, Mirabella saw her uncle coming toward them in the castle and her heart took a dive on the spot.

∾

RINA TOLD Dracolin all about Mirabella's uncle and what the princess had told them.

Dracolin glanced at her. "And you believe her?"

"I do, just as much as I believe that Vladek is evil."

"I can't believe you got yourself into this mess," Dracolin said. Then he smiled at her. "Then again, I can."

It was true she could be rather impulsive at times, but she always had good outcomes on her missions even if it seemed she'd had to make a detour to help her solve them.

They continued to travel toward the Castle Grande, but they weren't attacked any longer. Rina wondered why Vladek had a change in plans. Except that the princess was no longer with them, so possibly Vladek's elven knights had gone to King Leogane's castle instead. She voiced her opinion to her cousin.

"I hope not," Dracolin said.

Then they saw the dragon carrying Persephonice. Rina hoped that it meant the princess was safely within the walls of Castle Grande.

The dragon finally landed in front of the group of knights and Persephonice said, "I saw no sign of campfires or anyone in the vicinity."

So she had helped to scout for them too. That was good.

"Could they have made their way to Castle Grande?" Rina asked.

"I came from there. If they did, they were well hidden in the woods," Persephonice said.

"Will we make it there today?" Rina asked, wondering just how far away it was.

"Aye," the king said.

Dracolin dismounted the dark arts knight's horse and climbed onto the dragon with Persephonice. "We'll scout for them further. Rina, will you come with us?"

Rina figured he worried about her on the ground with the

other knights, which was ridiculous because she had so much backup when she didn't normally.

"You can help us look for them," Dracolin said, as if appealing to her need to help others, when she was sure he just wanted to protect her.

"Thanks, but I'll stay with the king and his men." Artur especially, Rina was thinking. She hadn't meant to look back at Artur and reveal how she felt about being with him and helping to protect him and the others in the party.

Then Dracolin smiled a little and the dragon rose up into the air and flew high above, swooping over the woods.

Rina hoped he would find the knights and the druids. She was afraid they might have headed for the king's castle instead.

"I'm glad you stayed with us," Artur told her.

"To protect you? I needed to stay with my horse."

Artur smiled.

She hoped he didn't think she had stayed because of him. With no sign of any of Vladek's knights, they finally reached the Castle Grande. She wasn't sure what to do now. Eat here? Sleep here, but then leave? The princess would safely be with the king and as long as she was happy here, Rina figured she wasn't needed.

She wasn't sure why, but she felt something wasn't right. She'd never been here before, so it wasn't like she would know if anything had changed. She turned to Artur, "Do you feel like something isn't right?" If anyone should know, it would be the people who lived here.

"Yeah. I hear a lot of activity within the castle walls, which seems strange when the king isn't there."

"Then maybe they are gathered to see the princess?"

"Inside the castle, certainly, but not out in the inner courtyard."

The portcullis had been closed, but it opened for the king

and his escort. But inside, another force was waiting for them. Not the dark arts knights, thankfully, but—She glanced at Artur to learn who these men were.

"King Inari's men." Artur shook his head.

"Oh, this is so not good," Rina said.

"I agree. It's not good at all if Princess Mirabella told us the truth about her uncle."

MIRABELLA HAD NEVER EXPECTED her uncle to arrive at Leogane's castle. But before she had to deal with him, she was glad she had told Callie all the trouble they'd had and of course Callie was at once concerned about her father, Erlig.

"When I left them, Erlig was fine." But Mirabella was surprised Callie hadn't asked about King Leogane, if she'd wanted to marry him. Maybe she was angry with him for going to see her and then bringing Mirabella back here, which would indicate he would wed her.

"I'm so sorry that King Inari arrived just before you did and wishes to speak with you."

Mirabella couldn't believe her uncle had Leogane fetch her from Castle Mayden and then come here. Why not just meet them there? If he thought he would be here to ensure she didn't tell Leogane what she knew was true about her uncle, he would have met her at Castle Mayden and made sure she didn't say anything to Leogane, or if she had, he would have contradicted her.

Callie had escorted the two of them to a sitting room to speak with each other while servants brought them mead to drink. Mirabella thought Callie was so sweet and perfect for the king. She was great at making her feel comfortable and she seemed to know just what it took to make the perfect hostess.

Callie left them alone to speak, but she also had a couple of servants standing by in case they needed any other refreshments.

Mirabella jumped in right away with questioning her uncle about Vladek and his men. "Count Vladek has sent druid-created dark arts knights to kill King Leogane and his men."

Her uncle's gray eyes smiled without humor. "Even this is wilder than any story you've ever made up before."

"Aye, well, once you speak with Leogane and the others he will confirm my wild story." And she prayed Leogane would realize she had told him the truth about her uncle. "Why are you here, Uncle?"

"This is my business, not yours."

Then Mirabella assumed Inari was there to speak with Leogane. Most likely to see if she'd behaved herself enough that Leogane planned to marry her. Goddess, she hoped Leogane would take her up on her offer to remove her uncle from the throne.

Callie suddenly appeared at the entryway to the room. "King Leogane has just arrived at the castle." She was all smiles like she was happy for Mirabella.

Mirabella just didn't understand her. She had even worried that if she married the king, Callie would create drama for her or even be his mistress. Maybe Callie was pretending to be fine with the situation because she knew she didn't have any choice in the matter.

Mirabella felt apprehensive about seeing Leogane now, and the way he would interact with her uncle and even with Callie. If Leogane treated him with respect, she was afraid she'd blow her top. She realized then she had to get Leogane in her court, at least while her uncle was here. She had to, or she could be in real trouble. What if Leogane said no to marrying her—and her uncle turned her over to Vladek? She knew he would too because he'd still want an alliance. She didn't trust her uncle would do what was right after Leogane told him what Vladek had done, or that he employed druids to make some kind of undead knights or whatever they were.

Her uncle took hold of Mirabella's arm as they walked to the great hall behind Callie, holding her arm so tightly in his grip, he had to have bruised her for sure, controlling as ever, and she hated him for it. But when Mirabella saw Leogane and their gazes connected, she saw something there, real feeling for her and he didn't even give Callie a glance. Callie hurried to hug her father, looking thrilled to see him back safely.

Rina and Artur were eyeing Inari with Mirabella, looking like they were ready to fight him. She figured they believed her about what her uncle had done.

King Leogane's gaze shifted immediately to Inari's grip on her arm, and he didn't appear to like it. "Come, join me at the table for a feast." He quickly joined Mirabella and her uncle and took hold of Mirabella's hand as if he'd decided he was going to marry her and pulled her away from her uncle.

Mirabella was so shocked, she hadn't expected anyone to do that for her. Her uncle planned to sit on the other side of Mirabella at the high table, but Leogane made him sit on the other side of him instead. It was the place of power, but she knew her uncle wanted to make sure she didn't say anything to Leogane that would ruin his reputation. It was a little too late for that. Rina and Artur sat next to Mirabella as if to protect her from her uncle and his men and she was grateful for that. For the first time since her father had died, she actually felt others cared about her welfare.

After toasting King Inari's unexpected visit, Leogane said to him, "I agree to wed Mirabella."

Mirabella's mouth gaped. She hadn't really expected Leogane to offer to marry her.

"Did you know about Vladek and his men?" Leogane asked Inari.

"Mirabella gave me some wild version of some fight you had, but like usual, she is full of wild tales."

"All she said was true," Leogane said, then ate some of the wild boar his people had prepared for them.

Mirabella looked at the king, wondering if he meant he believed everything she had said, even about her uncle killing her father?

Leogane leaned over and kissed her cheek, shocking her.

"I've decided to take Mirabella home with me to await your big wedding day," Inari said.

She couldn't go home with him. What if he beat her? Killed her? Her heart was racing; she felt panicked.

Leogane reached over and took her hand and squeezed. "We marry today. There is no need to wait."

"I insist," Inari said, glancing at Mirabella, telling her in no uncertain terms to tell Leogane she wanted to do as her uncle said.

But she wasn't that dumb. It appeared, if nothing else, she had a safe haven here.

Erlig and his daughter were seated on the other side of Inari and Callie didn't seem to be upset about Leogane's declaration of marriage to Mirabella. Mirabella still didn't know how to feel about all this.

If Mirabella married Leogane, would he go against her uncle then like she wanted him to?

"I'll gladly wed King Leogane," Mirabella said, figuring she truly had no choice if she didn't want to return with her uncle. What if he wanted to hand her over to Vladek instead of allowing her to marry Leogane? She wouldn't put it past her uncle. Vladek might not believe her or even care about what her uncle had done to her father. She doubted her father would have ever forced her to marry Vladek, given what she'd learned about him.

"I withdraw the offer of my niece in marriage to you," Inari said. "I've made a mistake."

"You would give Mirabella to the man who has druids working for him? And those druids that create creatures to fight us that turn to dust when dead?" Leogane asked Inari.

"It's my business what I do with my niece."

"You didn't have anything to do with—" Leogane said and Mirabella held her breath. She thought he was going to mention her uncle having her father killed. But then he continued, "Vladek's men fighting us, did you?"

"Why would I do that?" Inari sounded shocked that Leogane would come to that conclusion.

"Because you are now planning to offer her to Vladek." Leogane drank some of his mead.

Inari cleared his throat. "I didn't say I would."

"There is no one else for you to ally with," Leogane said. "If the princess's father had still been alive, he would have allowed the marriage with me to go through."

Inari glanced at Mirabella with hatred in his eyes. She couldn't eat. She was just too upset about everything.

"Callie, Rina, will you take Mirabella to her chamber? We will meet in the chapel as soon as Mirabella has dressed for the wedding." Leogane rose from the table.

Inari's face was red, and she'd never seen him so red faced when he hadn't gotten his way. "You will regret this," Inari said.

"You don't wish an alliance between us?" Leogane asked and Mirabella was afraid Leogane would change his mind about marrying her if her uncle didn't agree to it.

Rina took hold of her hand and squeezed it, reassuring her that Mirabella wouldn't return with her uncle no matter what happened between her and Leogane.

14

W hen the ladies arrived at the chamber assigned to Mirabella, it was just beautiful. Gold fabrics were draped over the window, tapestries of women and men dancing hung on the walls, a large bed with a canopy covered in gold sheers, and hand-carved, oak furniture covered in blue velvet cushions, so soft to sit on made up her chamber. It was such a drastic change from the tower room she had been confined to and she loved it here. She already felt welcomed and at home, something she had worried about. But truly, anything would have been better than where she'd been living.

All smiles, Callie said, "I'm so excited for you and the king. I'll be right back with your wedding gown." Then Callie left her alone.

"Are you all right with marrying the king?" Rina asked, while Callie was gone. She sounded concerned. "Is this what you want?"

"Aye. I know now he'll protect me from my uncle. After seeing my uncle again, which nearly made my heart stop, and the way he forced me to walk with him, his grip telling me to mind what I said to the king, though it was already too late for that, I suspected he had a change of plans for me. The only way to thwart him would be to marry Leogane and I truly want to do this. I believe he will be good for me. I do care about him already. He is a handsome man and protective. I just worry whether I will be able to fill the shoes of his queen. I've never been trained to take care of a staff or any other duties a queen might have." Mirabella truly worried about that. What if she couldn't manage? He would believe he'd made a mistake in marrying her.

"He's a good man," Callie said, returning with a dark-haired and eyed maid, who appeared a little overwhelmed, her eyes lowered, her hands clutched around the gown. "This is Franny. She'll help you also. You have me to help you with learning our protocols here and the king will be understanding. He's good that way."

Franny held out the beautiful pale blue gown covered in pearls.

Mirabella loved the gown. She had never seen anything more beautiful in her life. "Where is Justina?" She suddenly wondered what had become of the woman.

"She wasn't invited to eat at the great hall or to attend to you that I know of. I believe she ate with the servants in the kitchen. Would you like me to get her for you?" Callie asked.

"No," Rina quickly said. "She works for the princess's uncle. She isn't to be trusted."

Callie looked a little surprised that the warrior elf would answer for Mirabella, but already Mirabella had found a friend in Rina. All along, Rina had wanted to protect her, once she had learned her story about how she had been locked in the tower and needed rescuing, and Rina had believed Mirabella about her uncle.

"Don't you love the king, Callie?" Mirabella asked as they helped her out of her dusty traveling clothes.

Servants brought bathwater for her to bathe in and poured it into a tub, then left the chamber.

"I love another man. You might have met him on your trip here. Jeremka? But of course I would have married the king if he'd wished it. It would have been my duty," Callie said. "But I knew he didn't love me any more than I did him."

Mirabella sighed. She was so glad she wasn't destroying a love match. She hadn't wanted to do that.

When the maid lifted the tunic over Mirabella's head and they saw her back, Rina, Callie, and the maid gasped.

"Who has done this to you?" Rina asked, sounding as though she was ready to kill the person who had whipped her and scarred her back.

"My uncle." Mirabella no longer felt any pain there. She had forgotten about the scars that had long since healed, but she could not see them herself. She hoped Leogane didn't reject her for the ugly scars on her back.

"He doesn't deserve to live," Callie said. "I saw the way he held your arm with a death grip. King Leogane will not like seeing the bruises there."

"They are battle scars," Rina said. "You have been put into the most dangerous situations without a way to fight for yourself and have survived. The king will appreciate you even more for it."

Mirabella hoped Rina was right about it and loved that she was attempting to make her feel better about it. But any scars that Rina carried would truly have been due to fighting a battle so Mirabella didn't feel it was the same at all.

∼

RINA COULDN'T BELIEVE Mirabella's uncle had beaten her like that. Wouldn't the man who wed her realize her uncle was evil then? Then again, some men would do anything for more power, and they might even be as abusive as her uncle toward her if she didn't do as he expected of her.

Rina didn't believe Leogane would be that sort of man. She thought he would be good to her. Mirabella needed someone that was good for her after all these years of abandonment and threats. She suspected Leogane would be shocked to see that her uncle had hurt the princess like that.

After Franny washed Mirabella, Callie and Franny dried her off and dressed her. Rina was watching out the window, wondering what Vladek and his druids and their knights were doing. And what King Inari and his men were doing. Would Inari attend the wedding even though he had taken back his offer to have an alliance with Leogane when he wed Princess Mirabella? Not to mention Rina wondered what Artur was doing now too. She should have been with him and her cousin. She wasn't a lady's maid, but she had gone with her to her chamber, needing to know if Mirabella really wanted to marry King Leogane. Besides, the king had asked her to go with her, maybe even to protect her.

"I hope you will keep me on as your companion," Callie said to Mirabella.

"Oh, aye, I'm thrilled to finally have a friend."

"You will be queen," Callie said, as if she wanted her to know she couldn't be a friend like Mirabella had hoped for. "But I will be there for you always." She smiled.

"You will be my friend. Even a queen needs them. Just like Rina is my friend, though she is a powerful warrior. I mean, they can really make the best of friends, eh?"

Rina smiled, appreciating the princess for including her as a friend. "Titles mean nothing to me. So, aye, I will be your friend."

"You can even stay here with us. Be my bodyguard and friend?"

Rina laughed. "I have too many missions to accomplish for now." She didn't want to be in a stationary job like that, watching over the princess always. She had more adventures she wanted to go on. And getting rid of Vladek's druids remained a priority for her.

"I understand," Mirabella said. "I wish I could help you."

"You need to be here for yourself, for your new people, for the king," Rina said. She hoped Mirabella would find this to be a good home for her now. At least her accommodations were beautiful, inviting, perfect for a princess. Well, a queen soon.

"You will love it here," Callie said. "Everyone is eager to welcome you as their new queen."

Callie and the maid finished plaiting her hair, and then they seemed to take a collective sigh. "Are you ready to go to the chapel?" Callie asked.

"Aye." Mirabella sounded ready to get this over with. She looked nervous though.

Rina was glad she wasn't the one being put on the spot like this.

Just then Justina looked timidly into the bedchamber. "May...may I speak to the princess?"

"Certes," Mirabella said.

Everyone stayed there with Mirabella in case Justina was up to no good.

"I...I know you can hear things that most of us can't, and you might have heard my talk with King Leogane. I'm sorry for everything I said to King Leogane about you. Phiri told me to say those things to the king. Before I ask your forgiveness, I want to tell you I...I just told King Leogane the whole truth, that everything I had said to him earlier were lies. I...I don't want to work for your uncle. He's a bad man. From what I've seen concerning you, you've been a victim. If you can...can forgive me, I would like to work for you like I should have been doing all along." Justina looked like she truly was repentant. She was young. Maybe she could become a proper lady in waiting to the princess.

"Aye, I had hoped you could be," Mirabella said.

Rina hoped Justina wouldn't disappoint her, but the woman could be sent away if she didn't work out.

Callie stayed with Mirabella while Rina and Franny and Justina followed behind her. "The king will allow you to choose your own maids and companions."

"I'm glad. Will you help me since I know no one here?" Mirabella asked.

"I will."

That would be a big change for Mirabella, Rina thought, since her uncle had been the one who assigned the princess's guards and maids before that.

When they finally reached the chapel, it was filled with courtiers and the king was waiting for Mirabella, smiling, looking eager to marry her.

Such a change from when Rina had seen Mirabella and the king's interaction at Castle Mayden.

Artur joined Rina as she glanced around for Mirabella's uncle. "Where is he?"

"Her uncle? He was furious and left with his men," Artur said.

The ceremony was still going on when Rina looked for Dracolin and Persephonice in the gathered crowd in the church. Had they already left?

Artur leaned over and whispered to Rina, "Who are you looking for now?"

"My cousin and his wife."

Artur smiled at her. He pointed to them standing nearby,

watching the ceremony, like Rina and Artur should have been doing. Rina glanced around at the people in the chapel, seeing the smiles everyone was wearing. They appeared to be happy to have Mirabella there and that she was marrying their king. Rina was glad for that.

When Leogane and Mirabella kissed, it looked like the kind of kiss Rina would like to share with a man she loved. She smiled. She was happy for them.

Then the king and his wife headed out of the chapel where they would have a large celebration planned for the newly married couple. A coronation to make her his queen would come a few days later.

Artur asked Rina, "Were you like this when your cousin was married?"

"When Dracolin married Persephonice? What do you mean?"

Artur laughed. "Everyone else was quiet, watching the ceremony. You were full of questions."

Rina smiled. "I had to know what was going on with everyone."

"During the king's wedding ceremony."

She sighed. "I had to find out about everything. They look happy, don't they?"

"Yeah, they do."

"She needed someone like him in her life." Rina let out her breath, so bothered by the scars she'd seen on Mirabella's back when Rina figured she hadn't done anything to deserve it, she said to Artur, "Her uncle beat her."

Artur's eyes widened.

"She has scars on her back from his beatings."

Artur rubbed his chin. "The king doesn't know, does he?"

"I doubt he would unless Mirabella mentioned it and I don't think she would have talked to him about it. I wonder how

Leogane will take it."

"If he didn't believe her before about what her uncle did to her father, he will know it once he sees the abuse she has suffered," Artur said.

"You still don't know if he believes her?"

"He didn't talk to me about it, but after the way her uncle had hold of her arm and was dragging her with him, I'm sure she'll have bruises on her arm. King Leogane will have to figure her uncle was a bully and that the rest was true. What are you going to do after this?" Artur asked.

"Oh, I need to get rid of a couple of druids and Vladek who was trying to kill us also."

"I'm going with you. The king wants to send some of his men with us. Dracolin and Persephonice want to go with us."

"Good."

"I thought you liked to go alone on your missions," Artur said, sounding like he was teasing Rina.

"Normally, I do. But this time, I don't mind sharing the glory with you. As far as Dracolin going? There's absolutely no saying no to him."

Dracolin and Persephonice joined them then. "Are you ready to go?" Dracolin asked.

"Where?" Rina asked.

"To get rid of some druids. She's known as the Dark Arts Druid Slayer. Did you know?" Dracolin asked Artur.

Rina rolled her eyes at her cousin.

Artur smiled. "No, she didn't tell me that."

"She's killed three already. I haven't managed to find even one," Dracolin said.

"Three?" Artur glanced at Rina and she knew he'd be questioning her about the other two cases.

"We were going to the wedding feast," Rina said, figuring her cousin was giving her a hard time like he was known to do.

Those who were invited to a king's wedding feast didn't turn down the opportunity. It could look like a slight.

"You can stay for the feast. We're going," Dracolin said.

"No, I'm going. I'm just surprised. Ahh, you think that this is the best time to locate the druids and Vladek," Rina said.

"Yeah. They'll figure everyone's busy with the celebration. We don't doubt we'll see Inari with them, stirring up more trouble," Dracolin said.

"Are you scouting the area using the dragon?" Rina asked.

"No. We'll go by horse. The king is providing them to us," Dracolin said.

"So they know you're going to search for the druids while he's having his feast with his new bride?" Rina asked.

Dracolin smiled at her. "Of course. We wouldn't think of ditching the king's wedding feast otherwise."

"Okay, so what are we waiting for? And how many of the king's men are going with us?" Rina asked.

"This is it. You, me, Artur, and Persephonice. Of course you know of her ability to speak to creatures that we can't speak with. She will try and talk to the dark arts knights and see if she can get through to them, to turn them away from what the druids and Vladek are trying to have them do," Dracolin said.

"That would be great." Though Rina didn't believe Persephonice could control creatures that turned to dust upon death, if they were ever alive in the first place. But Rina had to look in on the married couple in the great hall just for a moment.

They were laughing with each other, and then dancing.

"You are a romantic. I never figured you would be," Artur said to her. "You owe me the stories about the other druids."

She smiled at him. "Just don't call me the Dark Arts Druid Slayer."

"I like the name."

"I do lots of other missions and I don't want everyone to think that's all I do."

Then they headed out into the courtyard, but Jeremka met up with them. "King Leogane said I could go with you also."

"Good," Artur said. "We can use your help."

Rina thought it would make it harder for them to sneak around, the more of them there were. Everyone was dressed in padded armor. She had thought of going without horses, but that would take them too long to reach the druids they were trying to locate.

15

The more Artur learned about Rina, the more he wanted to know. He figured when Leogane learned Mirabella had been physically beaten, he'd want to kill her uncle himself. Artur would be there helping him. But that Rina had killed two more druids and hadn't mentioned it to them? He had to know the stories.

The weather turned foul not too far from the castle, rain coming down in a torrent, the wind whipping about them. It could be a good thing for them though. It would muffle their horse's footfalls and help cover their tracks.

It was harder on them as they pulled their cloaks up to protect themselves from the cold rain.

They traveled for about five miles when Rina disappeared. Rina had left her horse or maybe she was on her horse, but just cloaked. Artur sure wished he had that ability.

∿

ALONE, Rina ran through the woods, seeing a dark arts knight, and blending with a tree, and when he disappeared, she began moving again. She knew she needed to run by herself and cloak herself every time she ran into one of the knights until she could locate Vladek and his druids. Going with her friends just wouldn't work as well. Once she found these guys, she'd return to her companions and let them know where they were.

Then she heard King Inari speaking with someone. His own men? She thought they would have been headed for their Black Hills castle, not here.

Then she heard Vladek talking. They were together. "You shouldn't have told Leogane that he could have the princess. If we had done what we agreed, you would have had an alliance with me."

"He and I have always seen eye to eye on who our enemies are. You were an unknown."

"But you told him you had changed your mind?" Vladek asked, sounding furious.

"Aye, like we agreed. But Leogane decided to marry her. What could I do then? I couldn't stop him," Inari said. "I told her he couldn't marry her, and he said he was going to anyway. He had the superior forces. I couldn't go against his wishes."

"Do you think he'll learn you killed Mirabella's father?" Vladek asked.

"What?" Inari sputtered. "Who said such lies?"

Rina moved closer to see them standing in the pouring rain, all huddled up. There were no dark arts knights in the area. Just a few of Vladek's elven knights and Inari's men and the two druids.

She wished she could take out one of the druids at least, but they were all too close together.

"You don't have to lie to me about it," Vladek said. "I know the truth. I don't care how you came to be on the throne. I just want your niece for my wife."

"And the alliance," Inari said, as if he wasn't sure if Vladek still wanted it.

"Of course. And the properties and coin as part of her dowry."

Rina had known the imposter healer had lied that Vladek hadn't wanted any of those things.

ARTUR SAW PERSEPHONICE suddenly slide off her borrowed horse. Now what?

She held up her finger to her lips and motioned to the woods. Dracolin dismounted and walked with her, protecting her. That's when Artur saw what they were doing. A dark arts knight was near them and Persephonice was speaking to him in a low, calm voice. Artur couldn't hear her words, but he was shocked to see the knight didn't immediately attack her.

At the same time, Artur kept watching for any sign of any more of the dark arts knights, wishing he knew where Rina was. She'd better not be going after the druids, Vladek, and Inari all on her own. He glanced back to see the dark arts knight move off as if Dracolin and Persephonice weren't the enemy. Artur had never seen Persephonice work her magic with creatures the elves couldn't communicate with. What had she told him and what was he doing? Would he keep their conversation quiet?

Artur could just imagine the knight returning to his master and telling him a woman had talked to him.

Persephonice and Dracolin returned to Artur. "What did you say to him?" he asked, his voice hushed.

Dracolin was waiting to hear too. He didn't have Persephonice's ability to understand other languages, so he wouldn't know what was said either.

"I told him he had new orders. He is supposed to tell the others like him to eliminate the druids," Persephonice said.

"Will he do it?" Artur couldn't believe she'd tell him to do that. It was a great idea—if it worked.

"He said he would. But the druids might be able to change his or the others' minds back to what they were supposed to do—eliminate Leogane and his people. I told him we were not Leogane's men, just travelers passing through. The knight said they wanted to end this. As it is, they are not alive, and they aren't dead. They fight because they are made to, but they only do as well as they can to appear to Vladek and his druids that they are doing his bidding. In truth, they can't wait to return to their former state where they were resting in peace. They have fought enough battles in their time."

"So they will aid us?" Artur asked.

"Yes, if he spoke the truth and I believe he did. He just needed new orders, which I gave him," Persephonice said. "Where's Rina?"

"I don't know. I'm afraid she is looking for their encampment," Artur said.

"Let's find her," Dracolin said.

RINA SAW a group of dark arts knights approach the campfire, walking right past her hiding place against a tree and in the heavy rain. She didn't think they could hear her frantic heart beating.

"What are you doing in camp?" Vladek asked, sounding surprised and angered. "You're supposed to be watching Leogane's castle."

Had they seen the companions leave the castle? It didn't make sense that they hadn't reported this to Vladek.

"Go," the druid Cabillero said, waving his arm in the direction of the castle. "You have your orders."

But the dark arts knights continued to move into the camp, their numbers growing. Inari looked shaken, his eyes wide, his hand on the hilt of his sword. It appeared Vladek had a revolt on his hands unless it was as the druids said. They'd make the dark arts knights more powerful, but at a cost. They could lose control of them. What if they attacked Inari and his men? It would serve the king and Vladek right.

Then one of the dark arts knights drew close to Cabillero and as soon as she saw him swing his sword at the druid, she couldn't believe it. At once, Vladek pulled out his own sword to kill the knight.

The next thing she knew, the knights were fighting Vladek's inner circle of elven knights, Inari's knights, and still trying to take down the druids. The dark arts knights had killed two of Inari's men and he appeared to be looking for a horse and a way to escape this.

Vladek was killing the dark arts knights now swarming into camp as quickly as he could. She didn't think the knights tired like the elves did after fighting an insurmountable number. The druids were trying to regain control of the knights and Rina knew she and her companions might have the upper hand in this moment. She rushed forth, moving from tree to tree, getting closer to the druids, seeing a dark arts knight look in her direction when she was visible in the gap between the trees. But none were bothering with her now. It seemed the druid's magic had backfired on them, but she couldn't risk them finally getting control of the situation.

She finally reached the clearing near where the first of the druids was located. Two of Vladek's elf knights were protecting him from the dark arts knights now. It was now or never. If she lunged forward to attack the druid, would the elf knights and the dark druid knights gang up on her? She had to try.

She dove into the melee, fighting one of Vladek's elf knights, hoping a dark arts knight wouldn't strike her in the back. She took the elf knight down and tore into the druid, killing him instantly. Before she could reach the other druid who was much farther away from her and in the midst of a chaotic battle between Inari's men, Vladek's elves, Vladek, and the dark arts knights, she saw Artur, Jeremka, and Dracolin coming to help her fight. Persephonice believed in instilling peace between warring factions, so Rina was a little surprised she was here. She wasn't fighting, but no one was attacking her either as she stood on the peripheral of the fighting, and looked as if she was surrounded by a protective shield. Rina had never seen it for herself, but she'd heard Persephonice could protect herself with one and had when the blue elves had tried to shoot her with blow darts filled with a sleeping potion.

Before Rina could reach the last of the druids, she was facing Count Vladek. He'd managed to get a horse and swung his sword at her, trying to strike her down. She swept up behind him onto the horse's back, blending in with the horse, and yanked Vladek hard, unseating him from his mount.

She leapt down, intending to take him into custody when she saw Artur dispatch the last of the druids. To her surprise, the dark arts knights all collapsed, and she guessed the druids had used a different spell to create them, unlike the other cases she'd dealt with. This was so not good. The other dark arts knights had continued to fight until the end and they'd remained the enemy. But this time, the knights had been on their side and now Rina and her friends had no army of their own. With only the four of them to fight Vladek, Inari, and the men they had left, Rina and her party were way outnumbered. They'd never last.

Vladek and Inari were smiling. They had them right where they wanted them. Vladek swung his sword at Rina and behind her, Dracolin, Jeremka, and Artur began to fight other elf knights.

Suddenly, dark shadows appeared against the sky, lightning revealing three dragons above. They swooped down and Dracolin and Persephonice leapt onto one of them. Vladek took advantage of the distraction and cut through the leather and padding protecting Rina's arm. Artur grabbed her by the waist and lifted her onto another dragon, the men all trying to reach them, but the dragon blew fire and the elf knights rushed back to avoid the white-hot flames.

Jeremka climbed onto the last dragon that incinerated a few archers who were trying to shoot the dragon riders and the dragons with their bolts before he flew off to join them.

"What exactly happened back there?" Rina asked Artur, holding her injured arm.

He hugged her close to him and to the dragon. "Persephonice convinced the dark arts knights to kill the druids. Except you killed one of them instead," Artur said.

"And you killed the other."

"Aye, but I didn't expect it to work out the way it did."

"With all the dark arts knights reverting to dust? Yeah, that was a shock. The ones in previous cases fought until they died. I really hadn't expected that. What about Inari and Vladek? They still live." Rina was in so much pain, she could barely think straight. And then she thought about her horse and theirs. She whistled, hoping her horse would guide the others back to the castle.

"They will have to manage with the elven forces and not their dark arts forces this time. We'll return to Castle Grande and the king will send his forces to fight them."

"And us."

Artur smiled at her. Seated upon the huge, green-scaled beast of a dragon, he kissed her in the pouring rain. "You will not fight. You're injured. It's time for you to enjoy the king's feast."

Rina shook her head. "I never celebrate until the mission is done. I always thought Persephonice was the most peaceful sort of person."

"She is. The dark arts knights were created out of darkness. They wanted to return to their resting place. She helped make that happen by turning them on those who had created them, giving us the chance to destroy the druids."

"You will now be called a dark arts druid slayer," she said, amused.

"So tell me about the other two druids you eliminated."

"You will think I'm bragging."

"If you were a braggart, you would have already told us about the others. As it was, you only revealed to us enough to let us know what we were up against."

She groaned in pain and then everything before her, the rain, the feel of Artur's warm body against her, his arm wrapped securely around her, all faded away.

ARTUR WAS TERRIFIED that Rina had succumbed to her wound but was glad Persephonice had called on the dragons to come to their aid or none of them would have made it out alive. He'd continued talking to Rina, trying to keep her awake, but when she passed out, he feared the worst.

As soon as he saw the castle off in the distance, he called out to Dracolin, "Rina was wounded. She has passed out."

"No," Dracolin shouted, and Artur knew her cousin was duly concerned.

Once the dragons landed in the courtyard, Artur saw her horse and the others had returned to the castle as he handed Rina down to Dracolin, wanting to take her to see the healer himself, but he knew her cousin wanted to take care of her since he was family.

Dracolin and Persephonice hurried inside the castle. Artur knew he needed to see the king and tell him what had happened. But he wanted to be with Rina, making sure that she was okay.

"What happened?" Leogane asked him while Mirabella hurried off to check on Rina.

Artur explained how Persephonice had used her abilities to suggest to the dark arts knight to convince the others to eliminate the druids. When he got to the part about the druids dying and the dark arts knights who had been fighting Artur and his companions' enemies turning to dust, Leogane frowned.

The king ran his hands through his hair. "I thought the dark arts knights would continue to live and fight whoever they were ordered to eliminate."

"That's what we thought. But maybe the druids used a different spell on them," Artur said.

"Aye. What happened to Rina?"

Artur expected the king to gather his men to fight Inari and Vladek at once, but he was glad he asked about her. "Vladek struck her when the dragons came to our rescue, distracting her. I want to see her before I lead our men out to fight Inari and Vladek."

"I'll go with you."

Artur really appreciated Leogane and was glad he served as the king's champion.

They went into the chamber where the king's healer was taking care of Rina. Her arm was bandaged, and she'd been given medicinal herbs in a drink. At least she had come to.

"How are you feeling?" Artur asked her.

"I'm ready to fight Inari and Vladek and their men."

Artur smiled at her, but then glanced at her cousin and the king to make sure they weren't going to agree with her.

"I hired her to protect Mirabella. So this is where Rina stays," the king said, smiling a little.

16

"I'm going after Inari and Vladek," Leogane said to Rina and the others gathered in the chamber where she would recover from her battle wound.

"Go with him. You're his champion. You can't do anything here for me," Rina said to Artur.

"We'll look after her," Mirabella said, and Persephonice agreed that she'd stay for her also.

"I'll go with you," Dracolin told the king.

The other men left, but Artur looked one last time at Rina, then inclined his head and hurried after the other men.

By the time Leogane, Dracolin, and Artur made their way to the great hall, Erlig had already gathered their men to do battle with Inari and Vladek and their men.

"Callie told me what Inari had done to Mirabella, to warn me not to appear shocked when I see the scars," Leogane said to Artur.

"Rina told me what had happened to the princess," Artur said.

His face an angry scowl, Leogane shook his head. "I will do worse to the cowardly murderer." He glanced back at Erlig. "Stay here with the rest of my forces in case Vladek or Inari think to attack our people here while we're trying to catch up to them."

"Aye, Your Grace." Erlig might want to go with them into battle, but he also knew how important it was that he stayed at the home front in case their enemies attacked them there.

Then Leogane headed outside with Artur and Dracolin and mounted their horses. The dragons were resting on beds of straw nearby. They were too large for Leogane's staff to give them a place to sleep in the stable, but they seemed content enough. At least the rain had stopped.

The men rode out beyond the castle walls and Artur and Dracolin guided them to where the encampment had been. By the time they reached it, Inari and Vladek and their elvish knights were gone.

"They split up," a scout reported. "Some went to the south, the others in a westerly direction."

"Who went which way?" Leogane asked.

Artur suspected he wanted to deal with Inari first.

Dracolin said, "Both forces are small. Maybe twenty men apiece. They thought they'd have their druids and their dark arts knights doing all their fighting for them so they didn't bring a large force with them."

"We have forty men, but I don't want to split our forces," Leogane said. "Which way did Inari go?"

It sounded like to Artur that Leogane's focus was to right a wrong done toward both Mirabella and her father. Artur worried though about letting Vladek get away, should he hire some other druids and create more troops.

Another scout hurried back to them. "Inari traveled south. But it appears that the notion Vladek and his men are heading in a westerly direction is a ruse. His forces are heading south now, and it looks like he'll be rejoining Inari's forces."

Leogane smiled. "Good. We head south then and overcome

their forces. Maybe we will have the advantage and have only one of the forces to fight if the other hasn't joined him already."

As they traveled through the woods, Artur stayed by the king's side, but he couldn't help but wonder how Rina was faring. He also hoped she didn't join them out here by slipping away unseen. He wouldn't put it past her. Even though her one arm was injured, she could fight just as well with the other.

RINA FOUGHT the sleepy effects of the drugs the healer had given her for the pain and to promote the healing of her wound. It made her think of the faux healer who had murdered the real healer near Castle Mayden. The princess, Persephonice, and the maid had sat with her for some time, quietly talking about Persephonice's and Dracolin's adventures as a nice warm fire glowed at the hearth.

Rina felt relaxed, safe, happy, yet she struggled against the feeling because she knew she should be with Artur and Dracolin and the king even, helping to fight the monsters in the woods. Then the room grew so quiet, Rina swore everyone had just vanished, the heartwarming fire still crackling in the fireplace. She thought of Mirabella on her wedding night once Leogane returned from battle. Goddess, Rina hoped he returned home just fine. The same with everyone else. Especially Artur who knew his duty yet seemed conflicted about leaving her behind.

She wondered if Vladek knew of any other dark arts druids he could call upon and then Persephonice would be needed to work her magic again. Rina worried about the king's reaction when he saw the scars on Mirabella's back. She thought about Callie's declaration that she loved Jeremka. Rina wondered if the king would give them his blessing to be married to each other.

Suddenly, Rina was thinking about the amount of money the king would pay her. He'd never mentioned an amount. Why she was thinking about that, she hadn't a clue. But then she was thinking about her parents, who could very well be worried when Dracolin and Persephonice didn't return with any news of her. Her thoughts were flip-flopping all over the place.

She still didn't feel as though she had done anything wrong exactly. Though she supposed some of the reason she hadn't told them where she was going on this mission was because she figured they wouldn't have approved her going based on just a rumor.

The room was dark except for the fire glowing nearby. She was wearing a pretty sleeping gown with an embroidered necklace and sleeves. When had she changed into something so elegant? It wasn't hers. She sat up in bed and she felt dizzy, her arm shrieking in pain. Gods. She should never have let up her guard when she'd been fighting Vladek. She pulled aside the bed linens and saw her bags on the floor near a chair. Good. At least she could change into something more like what she was used to wearing. The problem was trying to dress with an injured arm. Pulling on her boots was the worst. Then she finally finished dressing.

No matter what anyone said, she had to join the fight. This was her destiny. She wasn't sure if anyone would let her out of the castle though. And if she couldn't leave with their permission, she sure couldn't take her horse. Fine. She'd climb over the wall and down the other side, and if she found one of the dark arts knights' horses left behind, she'd ride him to the place where she needed to be. She was not a highly trained warrior elf for no reason. She heard someone walking down the hall outside the chamber and she quickly climbed into bed and covered herself with the quilts and furs, but whoever it was walked on past.

Then Rina climbed back out of bed, determined to help her cousin, Artur, and the king in dealing with Vladek and Inari and their men.

She finally made it to the stairs and down them, seeing only one servant who was headed in a different direction and hadn't noticed her.

Then she slipped out into the inner bailey and headed to the wall walk. She climbed the stairs and watched for the guards at their outposts. No one was right there, and she slipped over the wall and began her climb down, just liked she'd done at the tower where she'd first seen Princess Mirabella. Though with her injured arm, it was painfully slow going and she slipped twice, nearly giving her a heart attack.

Fog now enveloped the area in a cloak of thick white mist. She wished she had her horse, but she could run to catch up to the men in time. She kept listening to any sounds that they might be engaged in a battle, but the woods were still, except for the bugs chirping in the night.

She first went to Vladek and Inari's encampment to see where everyone had gone to from there. She knew Leogane and his men had traveled to here first, doing the same thing she was doing. Their tracks were all over the place. No one was there now. And no other battles had been fought. The armor of the dark arts knights had been left behind. The dead elven warriors had been taken with Vladek and Inari, it appeared. But she noticed some of the men had left in one direction and the other men had left in a different direction. Still the freshest tracks were from Leogane and his men and they had headed south. She took off that way when she thought she heard something behind her, sneaking up. She whipped around, pulling out her sword, and hurting her injured arm. She cried out. That was not the way to prepare to fight her enemy. But she didn't see anything for a moment.

Then something moved, mostly hidden by the leaves and trees and she realized it was the dragon she and Artur had flown on to the castle earlier. Because she was part high elf, she could understand the dragon's language, thankfully. Her mother was the one who had the ability.

"What are you doing out here?" she whispered. She didn't think she needed to, but just in case any enemies were lurking about, she wanted to be cautious.

"I had the same question for you."

"I'm doing what a warrior would do. My job."

The dragon snorted, letting out a puff of mist. "Even warriors who are injured need time to heal and rest."

"You followed me out here?" She was surprised, glancing around, not seeing any of the other dragons with him. "Alone?"

"Yes. On my own. We had to decide among ourselves who would bring you back to the castle."

She shook her head. "I'm going to search for the men."

"Then I'll stay with you."

"You're..."

"Too big? You don't have a horse to ride like everyone else. I'll take you to where they are before they are in battle, but if Dracolin says you must be returned to the castle, I'll take you."

"You are?"

"Darksmoke." He laid down so she could climb onto his back.

She hesitated, but she knew if she didn't do it, he might just grab her in his talons and forcibly return her to the castle. She climbed onto the dragon's back, hoping they'd find the men soon. At first, Dragonsmoke flew in the direction she assumed the men had gone, but then the dragon changed direction.

For a while, she didn't say anything, figuring Darksmoke's hawk-like eyesight could see something she was missing—a campfire, movement in the woods, something. But then Darksmoke turned toward the castle. She didn't believe the men had ended up back there. She felt Darksmoke had tricked her then.

"Where are you going?" she asked, trying not to sound so irritated with him.

"To Castle Grande."

At least he was being honest with her.

"Why? I need to assist the others to fight Vladek and the rest of our enemies."

"You need to heal up, like I said before."

She let out her breath in exasperation. When she saw the castle, she figured she was going to be confined to her bedchamber this time. She was so disappointed, but her arm was killing her, and she figured—as much as she hated to admit it—she should stay there and recuperate some more.

As soon as he landed in the courtyard, Princess Mirabella, Callie, and Persephonice hurried to see her. "You are supposed to be in bed sleeping," Mirabella said right away.

Persephonice thanked Dragonsmoke for finding Rina and bringing her back to the castle.

"Traitor," Rina said to the dragon.

He responded with a puff of smoke, looking totally satisfied he'd done what he'd gone to do.

Persephonice just shook her head. "All three of them told me right away that you had left."

All three dragons smiled at Rina.

17

Artur and King Leogane and his men felt they were getting closer to their enemies. Inari's men were talking up ahead as if they knew no one would be following them, which was a mistake on their part. But it was good for Artur and their party. Vladek and Inari and their men were heading for Castle Grande and Artur couldn't believe it. Did they think they could lay siege to the castle? On the other hand, maybe they thought they could wait for more of their troops to arrive. Maybe even Inari believed he could regain entrance to the castle with his men, pretending to have a change of heart and want to celebrate the wedding of his niece to Leogane. He would pretend to offer an alliance, anything to get inside the castle walls again so that he could have his men kill the guards and open the portcullis to let Valdek's men in when everyone was asleep.

Not far from the castle, they found King Inari and his force waiting for Vladek's to arrive. This worked even better for Leogane's force because they could tackle Inari and his men before Vladek's reinforcements reached them.

It didn't take long before Leogane and his men were battling

Inari and his warriors. Artur saw Leogane going after Inari. Artur joined him so he could fight anyone who tried to attack his king.

The men from both sides were fighting each other to the death. Even though Leogane's force was larger, they knew at anytime Vladek and his men could arrive. Then what? They would be fresh in battle to fight them.

Artur was fighting two knights at once, wondering why it seemed everyone was ganging up on him when Leogane's side had the superior number, not Inari's men. Artur finally got the upper hand with one of the men, and the knight fell to his knees, then collapsed. The other man jumped in to take his place, but at least for Artur it was only the one this time.

They fought, swords clashing, sweat beading on Artur's forehead underneath his helm. He continued to fight just as aggressively as his foes, parrying, lunging forward, striking sword against sword, sword against shield, until he finally managed to get the advantage of the man. He killed the knight and then looked around at the battlefield, all the knights fighting in earnest, each one trying to protect himself and take down his enemy first.

Some of Inari's men had rushed forth to protect their king, and now Leogane was fighting some of those men. Artur and Jeremka hurried to assist him, and Leogane was grateful for that. But then they heard the charge of Vladek and his men and knew that they had raced to join Inari's men and fight against Leogane's, most likely hearing the battle from afar.

Both Leogane and Inari had lost a few men either to injuries or death and all of them had been fighting for the entire time. With the insurgence of the new forces, they could have the advantage. On the one hand, Artur wished that Rina was here with him, fighting side by side. On the other hand, he was glad she was safely back at the castle recuperating.

He was fighting some of Vladek's men now too when he saw
a figure suddenly appear beside him. He turned to look to make
sure it wasn't one of his foe. Rina? What the—?

Rina, her one arm bandaged, sword in her hand, swung it at
one of Vladek's knights and then she took him down and saw
Mirabella's uncle, but Leogane was fighting him again.

Rina might have been injured, but she fought like any knight
who hadn't been injured, with ferocity and determination to
take down the enemy. She was a warrior elf who was just as
skilled at fighting as Dracolin, though her cousin glanced in her
direction and scowled at her for being there.

She shouldn't have been there, but Artur understood why
she was. She was a fighter and she felt she needed to help their
side.

She killed another of Vladek's men, bumped into Artur's hip
once, but when he had a chance to look at her again, she had
vanished. He glanced at the ground, afraid she'd fallen, but she
wasn't on the ground. Where had she gone to now?

That's when he looked around the battlefield and saw
Vladek fighting Jeremka and the next thing he saw was Rina
thrusting her sword at Vladek also.

Goddess, Artur had to get over there now. He fought through
the crowd of men, seeing Jeremka turn to fight another Inari
knight at his back. Another of Vladek's knights struck at Artur.

Now Rina was fighting Vladek on her own. Dracolin
dispensed with the knight Artur was fighting. That gave Artur
the chance to move in Rina's direction again. She was tenacious.
He'd give her that.

Then he saw the three dragons moving in overhead.
Everyone was so busy fighting, no one saw the dragons until
they began grabbing Inari's or Vladek's men with their long
talons and carrying them off, reducing their knights' numbers.
Artur was getting closer to Rina when she fell. His heart practi-

cally gave out as he rushed past knights attempting to engage him. All he saw was Rina on the ground, trying to defend herself from the brutal attacks of Vladek, a much larger, muscular man. She couldn't camouflage herself with the ground because he was striking at her incessantly.

As soon as Artur reached Vladek, he struck at him, forcing him to fight him until Rina could get to her feet. She finally slowly stood, looking worn out while he was fighting Vladek. Artur realized his own shoulder was bleeding. He hadn't noticed it at first, but he wasn't stopping the fight between him and Vladek if he could help it. Rina cut Vladek in the arm and with the distraction, Artur thrust his sword into the count's chest a moment later. Vladek's eyes were wide, then he fell on his face to the ground.

Rina checked his pulse. "He's dead." She frowned. "You're hurt." She hurried to get something out of her pack and wrapped his shoulder.

For a few minutes, the fighting continued until some of Vladek's knights saw that the count was no longer leading them. Some of his elvish knights began to break off from the fighting and tore away from the battlefield. It appeared this was Vladek's fight alone, not theirs. Artur wanted to cheer, but he glanced around to see what was going on with Inari. He was dead, Leogane standing over his body and the fighting finally stopped.

The rest of Vladek's men immediately took off. The rest of Inari's men were taken into custody. They would either serve Mirabella and Leogane, or they would die. They couldn't have elvish knights in their camp who were still their enemy and would want to kill Leogane and his men.

Leogane's people cheered in victory, but then began gathering their injured and dead.

Because Inari had murdered Mirabella's father and stolen the crown, he would not be returned to the Black Hill's kingdom for a formal burial but buried here where he had fallen. They would leave no tombstone over his grave. He didn't deserve any more than that. Inari's knights would dig the trenches for their fallen and for Vladek and Vladek's dead also, since their own people had left them behind to save their own skins.

Artur pulled Rina into his arms and held her tight. "Are you all right?"

"Aye. But you've been wounded also."

He didn't bother to mention she shouldn't have been out there to fight when she was still healing from her wound. He didn't need to. Dracolin was right there, coming to their aid, or to scold his cousin.

"I would ask what you're doing here, but it's of no use," Dracolin said to Rina, almost as if he were scolding her, but he sounded like he was more resigned to it than annoyed.

Artur smiled at the two of them.

"You needed my help," Rina instantly said.

Dracolin called to a man who brought her a horse. Artur helped her onto it. "Aye, always." Artur found his horse and climbed onto it.

"I'm going back with you," Dracolin said, another man bringing him a horse.

They didn't need Dracolin's assistance in burying bodies or safeguarding prisoners. He had only been there to help them fight. Artur figured Dracolin was also making sure his cousin returned safely to the castle.

Jeremka stayed to help Leogane monitor things there since Artur had been injured and needed medical care.

They rode toward Castle Grande and Rina was gritting her teeth, keeping her injured arm close to her body. Artur saw blood on the bandages on her arm and hoped she hadn't been cut again. Even reopening the wound could be bad.

The dragons were carrying Leogane's wounded men back to the castle so they would receive medical care more quickly.

As soon as they arrived at the castle, Princess Mirabella, Callie, and Persephonice were there helping others to take care of the injured. Mirabella immediately came to Artur and Rina's aid.

"King Leogane is fine. He's uninjured," Artur said, knowing she'd want to learn of that first.

"Oh, good. Jeremka?" Mirabella asked.

"Aye, he's fine," Artur said.

Callie looked immensely relieved.

Mirabella ushered them into the castle as if she had quickly learned how to take charge of situations and he loved seeing that. She wasn't a spoiled princess at all.

She took them to the sitting room and a healer soon came into the room carrying herbs and supplies. She cleaned their wounds and wrapped them in bandages as Mirabella helped her and learned how to properly take care of the injured.

"What about my uncle?" Mirabella finally asked.

"He is dead," Leogane said, coming into the room and taking her into his arms and hugging her.

Tears filled her eyes.

"I would have taken him prisoner and made him stand trial, but he wasn't going to allow it. It was either kill me or die so we ended up fighting to the death," Leogane said.

"I'm glad he's gone. He deserved as much for what he did to my father and my people. Now what do we do?" Mirabella asked.

Leogane kissed her. "Now you become queen in his place, and you'll be queen here."

Mirabella smiled through her tears. "And you'll rule beside me as king."

"Aye. We'll put Erlig in charge here while we make the transition with your people and make sure they know who rules," Leogane said.

She nodded.

Then Leogane glanced at Artur and Rina. "Thanks to both of you for aiding us when we truly needed the assistance."

"Aye," Artur said, "as it should have been for me, but Rina—"

"Was needed also," she quickly said.

Mirabella smiled at her. "Once Darksmoke brought you back and we made sure you had returned to bed, we didn't think we'd have to post a guard to keep you there."

Rina shook her head. "I would have found a way to slip out."

"Through the window. Aye. Now will you be returning home?" Mirabella asked.

Dracolin walked into the room and said, "Aye."

"Nay. I mean, certainly, but only after I have enjoyed a feast. I keep missing out on them," Rina said.

They laughed.

"We will have one in the morning after you and the remainder of our party have rested up," Leogane said.

"What of that horrible woman at Mayden Castle. Phiri?" Rina asked. "And the guards there?"

"They will all be fired. They will have to make their way in the world. I don't intend to give them a chance to prove their loyalty to me like I will Justina." Mirabella smiled at Rina.

"Good," Rina said.

Artur was glad for that, and he realized Mirabella had the fortitude to make decisions like a queen would do.

Dracolin cleared his throat. "I meant to tell you that another langolar arrived near where Persephonice was left by the cliffs along the ocean. Word reached us before we returned home from our own mission, and then we had to come searching for you. We don't know any more than that."

"She has come to take her home?" Rina asked, sounding shocked and ready to defend her.

Persephonice joined them in the sitting room. "Are you all right, Rina? You weren't supposed to slip away like you did."

"I'm fine. What of this langolar that has come to our lands? Is she going to try to convince you to return to your ship and your father?" Rina asked.

"Nay, Persephonice stays with the shadow elves. With me." Dracolin folded his arms.

"Aye, I would never leave here. They say the langolar is a male this time. He disappeared, once the blue elves had spied him and the word spread to us that another of my kind had been left in the elves' world. Maybe the blue elves have taken him prisoner." Persephonice shrugged. "We don't know anything more about it than that. He may be someone I know, but we don't know his name."

Artur looked at Rina. She smiled at him. He wanted to growl. She had already said she might be interested in a male of Persephonice's kind.

"We will leave after the feast tomorrow then," Dracolin said, giving Rina a stern look, telling her she wasn't delaying returning home with them any longer.

"Of course. I wouldn't want to worry my family."

"Now you say so," Dracolin said.

"I'm going with her," Artur said, then realized he should have at least asked his king's permission! "To make sure that her family understands that she was very much needed to help with the princess's safety and further take down the druids, dark arts knights, Vladek, Inari, and their men."

Dracolin could tell her parents about a lot of what had gone on, though Artur had been there with her every step of the way.

Everyone was smiling.

"With your permission, of course, Your Grace," Artur quickly said to King Leogane.

"I would have suggested it if you had not offered," the king said with a twinkle in his eye.

"We will have to visit your land one of these days," Mirabella said. "Oh, and I told you I would pay for your services, Rina, once I had rule of my castle and the treasury."

"As did I," Leogane said.

Rina let out her breath and smiled. "Good. That should make everyone happy when I return after a job well done, money besides, and enough even to pay the shadow elf king's taxes."

THE NEXT DAY after resting up, they feasted to their hearts' content in the great hall, and it was finally time for Rina and her family to return home, accompanied by one determined knightly champion, Artur.

"You know you could be one of us," Artur said to Rina, riding beside her on their horses while Dracolin and Persephonice soared up above, watching for any signs of any other kind of trouble. "A champion serving King Leogane and his queen."

Two more dragons—the one called Darksmoke and the others—were flying nearby them. Artur and Rina could have ridden a dragon also, but she wouldn't leave Midnight behind, and Artur wouldn't leave his horse, Windstorm, behind either.

"You could be one of us. A warrior elf who is much needed all over." Rina turned to smile at him.

Artur had made this trip with thinking of doing just that, but he'd had to propose she could be in Leogane's forces also, in case she preferred that. He didn't have any living family, but she had her family who would most likely miss her too much and she the same with them if she moved far from home.

That night, they camped under the stars with three dragons surrounding them. The dragons had even caught fish for all of them, though they'd eaten theirs raw. Over the campfire, Dracolin and Rina cooked the rest of the catch for the elves to eat.

Once the meal was cooked, they ate their fish and their bread, and drank their mead.

"Expect Rina's father to ask a ton of questions of you when we arrive at the shadow elf kingdom," Dracolin warned Artur. "He would in general because they tend to rehash missions with the whole family to see what they've learned from the experience. But since you've come with us, he'll want your perspective on what went on."

"I'll be happy to fill him in on everything," Artur said, though he suspected her father would want to know why he had really gone there with them.

Then they cleaned up afterward and set up tents to sleep in. Artur kept smiling at Rina, hoping she'd just forgo sleeping in her own tent and stay with him, but she only smiled back, knowing just what was on his mind and she wasn't going for it.

The next morning, they had breakfast of oats and honey, then headed out again. "We'll get there late today," Rina said.

"It would be faster if we flew," Dracolin added.

"Aye, but I don't want to send Midnight home alone. If my folks saw him, they would think the worst. That I was in trouble, and they'd come after me," Rina said.

"Of course."

Then they were on their way, stopping to give the horses and dragons breaks, getting lunch, then heading out again. At least they hadn't had any trouble with any wildlife or hostile elves on the way.

As soon as they reached the village and the castle grounds of the shadow elves, several elves came out to welcome Dracolin and the others in the party. The sun hadn't faded yet and he was glad they had finally reached their destination.

Dracolin and Persephonice probably always had a warriors' welcome when they returned home because of the importance of the missions they went on. Several people were looking over Artur, the stranger in their midst. They were curious about him, and Rina quickly introduced him to everyone.

Then a dark-haired, dark brown eyed man and woman joined them, both having Rina's smile and slim build, both welcoming Rina home with hugs, then doing the same with Persephonice and Dracolin.

"You brought her home wounded," Rina's dad said, frowning at Dracolin.

"She was as safe as she could be under the circumstances." Dracolin told them all about their adventures, except he left out the fact that Rina was supposed to be on bedrest in a chamber at Castle Grande and had slipped out to fight—twice.

Rina's father looked at Artur and she quickly introduced him to her parents. He knew her parents were so relieved to see her that she had forgotten to mention him right away.

Her brother and sister soon joined them. They were just as dark haired as Rina, but both had dark brown eyes like their parents. Artur wondered how Rina had ended up with a green and a blue eye. They were remarkable and every time he looked at her, he would be lost in her gaze.

Rina put her arm around him, in a way that said she wanted to be with him.

"We were worried sick—" her mother said, clearing her throat when she saw how intimate Rina was with Artur.

"I am here to explain why Rina was with us, aiding us," Artur said.

Her father frowned at him. "It appears there's a lot more explaining that needs to go on, more than just her leaving to take care of a mission."

Her mother laughed. "It looks to me like you've already found your match. The question is are you staying with us or returning to Castle Grande?"

Rina turned to see what Artur had to say.

HER FATHER PUT his arm over Artur's shoulder and pulled him away from Rina before Artur could say whether he was staying with the shadow elves for good. She suspected Artur was going to get her father's lecture, tons of questions, and the king's champion might just decide it was safer to return to Castle Grande.

Rina glanced in the direction her father and Artur had gone, and she said to her mother, sister, brother, her cousin, and Persephonice, "Excuse me." She had it in mind that Artur might just need her protection again. But when she reached the location where her father and Artur were, they were sitting on bamboo chairs at the pond, drinking mead and talking about their many adventures.

Rina smiled. "I thought you were going to question Artur all about himself."

"He has no family, he's very much intrigued with your skill as a warrior and had to remove his armor to fight as a warrior like we do. He protected you and you protected him. What's more to say?" her father said.

Rina let out a relieved breath.

"What? Is there more he's not telling me?" her father asked sternly, but with a smile in his expression.

She sat beside Artur and patted his leg. "No." She was just glad no one had mentioned she had slipped away from the bedchamber after she had been wounded to help Artur and her cousin fight their enemy.

Before long, her mother, siblings, cousin, and Persephonice joined them.

"When you tell King Leogane that you are working with our family and courting Rina, how do you think he'll react?" her father asked Artur.

Artur smiled. "King Leogane is wise in all things, and he would only have said I could leave there to accompany Rina here, if he'd been willing to let me go permanently."

Dracolin said, "Aye, he knew where this was going from the beginning. Just like he said you knew where things would go between him and Mirabella."

"That seemed so long ago," Artur said.

18

"We have a new outsider here. But this time, he's a warrior," Rina's father said.

"We heard," Rina said. "Is he going to try and take Persephonice back to her father's ship?" That had been the reason for Eloria's coming here. She was supposed to convince Persephonice to go with her back to her ship. But Eloria had married instead and remained with the elves.

"We don't know. We heard he escaped the blue elves and then ended up in our territory. Would you like to meet him?" her father asked.

"Aye," Rina said.

"I do," Persephonice said. "I have to know if it's someone I recognize."

"Here I thought you wanted to be with a handsome langolar warrior type if a male ever showed up," Artur said.

"He's truly a warrior?" Rina asked.

Artur smiled at her.

"He was armed, if that indicates that he is," Rina's father said.

They all went to the town square where shadow elves were checking out the langolar.

As soon as Artur saw him, he frowned and drew closer to Rina, even taking hold of her hand. She glanced at him and smiled warmly. "What? You're not worried I'd be interested in the blond-haired, blue-eyed stranger, are you?"

Artur released the breath he'd been holding. "Of course not." But as soon as they walked over to meet him, Artur said, "Rina is with me."

Rina laughed and squeezed his hand. "Once I met you, no one else fascinates me like you do."

"Good."

"So are you going to try and convince Persephonice to return to the ship to her father?" Rina asked the langolar.

"No. I'm Orion," he said. "I came here because I had to know what the elves' world is like since she and her friend Eloria never returned to the ship. It sounded like a world worth visiting."

"Do you have the bracelet to return to your ship? The transporter bracelet?" Rina asked.

Orion smiled. "No. I ditched it in the ocean, hoping it wasn't a bad idea if the people here were hostile."

"Oh, we're hostile," Rina said, wrapping her arm around Artur's waist. "We're always ready for any battle, great or small."

Dracolin and Persephonice joined them then and Persephonice said to Orion, "So exactly why did you come here?"

"Your father sent me to forcibly take you from here and return you to the ship, which I willingly volunteered to do. But of course I had nothing of the sort in mind. My father and grandfather were great explorers and that's what I want to be," Orion said.

"Good. You will have many different creatures to meet and

much land and diversity to explore. Just do not make any enemies of those I have befriended," Persephonice said.

Then Rina and her family left the square to have a meal together. Rina asked Persephonice, "Do you trust Orion?"

She gave Rina a smile that said she didn't. If he had one of those wristbands, he could transport Persephonice to the ship without her approval. Rina noticed then a couple of armed guards were watching Orion.

"Dracolin is taking Orion for a dragon ride tomorrow." Persephonice didn't say any further.

Rina wondered if he planned to leave him off somewhere far away from the shadow elf kingdom to explore to his heart's content. It could be dangerous, but if Orion's father and grandfather were explorers, Orion would know that better than anyone.

"Do you know him?" Artur asked.

"No. We could live on a spaceship for years and not meet everyone. People get off to do assignments at different planets and sometimes never return to the ship or leave on others." Persephonice looked at Rina. "So what about you and Artur?"

Rina's brother called Artur over to help them cook the boar for supper. Artur headed over there and was laughing at something her brother was telling him and her father.

"I will be taking him on missions with me from now on, unless someone else in the family feels they need to mentor him," Rina said.

After a while, Artur joined her and hugged her. "I came here to be with you. I will go with you on the missions."

She glanced back at her father and her brother, wondering why Artur was no longer cooking the meal, but they were already serving up the boar on the outdoor table.

On evenings like this with the moon shining brightly, a warm, mild breeze blowing, it was perfect for an outdoor celebration.

Since Dracolin's father was Palmoran, the advisor to the shadow elf king, Dracolin and Persephonice usually just ate with him at his place of honor at the king's side.

Dracolin soon joined them, and they sat down to eat. "I was making arrangements for Orion's trip tomorrow. He is being guarded tonight at the castle and I'll pick him up in the morning."

"Are you sure you don't want me to come along?" Persephonice asked.

She and Dracolin were inseparable now.

Dracolin shook his head. "I don't want to risk it."

Rina didn't blame Dracolin. He'd fallen in love with Persephonice in the very beginning. Rina had hassled him about it, but in the end, she knew that the strange outsider had been the only one for him.

"You know Pascale is furious that you brought the knight home with you," Rina's brother said.

"You've got to be kidding me. He was seeing at least two other girls behind my back," Rina said.

Arthur ran his hand over Rina's arm consolingly. "Just say the word—"

"And you'll fight him?" Rina asked. "We'll have much more important missions to do than bothering with him."

Just then, Pascale showed up at their campfire, to Rina's irritation. Her father was on his feet in an instant, followed by Artur—though he didn't know who the man was—her brother, and Dracolin.

"Leave here at once, if you know what's good for you," her father said.

Rina could fight her own battles, but in this case, she loved all the men in her life for standing up for her and making sure the ex-boyfriend didn't bother her any further.

Pascale glowered at Artur for the longest time and then finally left.

The conversation about other matters started up again, but Artur said to Rina, "You never told me you had issues with some former boyfriend who was dallying with other women."

"I didn't feel I needed to. It was over and done with between us before I left to rescue a princess. I never expected him to be so bold as to show up here and try to, well, I don't know what he thought he'd do." Rina took a bite of her pork.

"Claim you? See his competition?"

She smiled. "He will never be your competition. A king's champion who was there to protect me against the hordes of our enemy? No, he had lost out when he started seeing the other women before I left on my mission."

IT WAS LATE that night as everyone had eaten and cleaned up after their family feast, regaling Artur of their wild adventures while he shared his too. Dracolin and Persephonice finally excused themselves to bid everyone a good night. As a newly married couple, they needed time to themselves.

"We have a cabin you can use until you find a place of your own," Rina's father said.

She was glad her father would offer for Artur to be there near them and not have to figure out a place to live until he knew what he wanted. Though she was certain Dracolin and Persephonice would have had him stay with them if her father had not offered the cabin.

"We all have missions to go on tomorrow, except for Rina and Artur," her father said. "That'll give you both a day to rest up before you go out again, especially since you're both recovering from your injuries."

She wondered if Dracolin and Persephonice had a mission too, other than Dracolin dropping Orion off in the wilderness. They had left before she had thought to ask.

"I'll walk you over there, Artur." Rina and he had stabled their horses earlier in her father's stables and they walked to the cabin that was just beyond that in a small clearing in the woods. "If you need anything, just let me know." Then she wrapped her arms around his neck, and he settled his hands on her hips and they kissed.

"How long do we need to court before we can stay together?" Artur asked.

Rina laughed. "If my father had a say in it, he would tell us you would have to wait a year."

Artur raised his brows. "But if not?"

"My parents were married within three weeks of meeting each other. Of course that had something to do with her being a high elf and they didn't want anyone saying she couldn't marry a shadow elf."

"Anyone?" Artur asked.

"Her parents, the king even, but everyone came around and they've been happily married for twenty-three years."

"How did they meet?" Artur asked.

"Oh, that's a long story. The high elves and the shadow elves were fighting each other. It doesn't happen very often, but it had to do with fishing rights over a mountain-fed river. The high elves live in the mountains, and they had claimed that many of the large tributaries came straight from the mountains. The shadow elves had claimed that the river ran right through their forests. Both were correct.

"During the fight, my mother used her ability to carry an object, or person in my father's case, and dumped him in the river. My father was leading the charge on that section of the river. When he looked to see who had done such a thing to him as he swam to shore, he saw my mother. She was smiling and he laughed. His laughing won her over. Her smile had won his heart."

Artur laughed. "And the fight?"

"Oh, it went on for days, no one making any progress until they decided to call it a draw and agreed to each of them fishing there. At that point, my father started to date my mother, secretly at first, and then openly. They've loved each other ever since."

"So for us how long will we court?" Artur asked.

"Oh, we'll have to see."

"I won't be like your last boyfriend, if you're worried about that."

She smiled, hating to admit that she did worry about that. All the single women here would be interested in the king's champion. What if one of them intrigued Artur more than she did? One that suited him better? Rina didn't have any false notions concerning that. Though she also figured if one of them approached him, batting her eyelashes at him, Rina might have to rein in her warrior elf training to avoid any complications.

They kissed each other good night again, and then she left him alone before her father came looking for her. But when she retired to her own bed, she was thinking about just how many weeks it would be before she married the king's champion. She didn't think she'd be able to hold out for very long.

BEFORE ARTUR WAS FULLY AWAKE, someone was pounding on his door that morning, and he wondered what all the fuss was about. Oh, breakfast. Maybe the family all ate breakfast together before they headed out on their missions. "Coming!"

He hurried to dress and went to the door to find Rina

standing there with their horses in tow. "Hurry up. We'll be late."

"For what? Breakfast?" But he couldn't imagine riding his horse somewhere to have breakfast.

"You slept through breakfast. Father said to leave you be, but Dracolin came to me with a mission since everyone else already had one. And he couldn't take it because of Persephonice."

"What mission?" Artur asked, grabbing his pack.

"Orion thinks he can communicate with all the creatures in our world. He can't. Some are just too...primitive. In any event, he's in trouble and we have to rescue him." She climbed onto her saddle.

Artur didn't like the sounds of that. What if Orion fell for the shadow elf, his Rina, who was coming to his aid?

As soon as Artur was on his saddle, she tossed him some fresh baked bread. "Your breakfast."

"Thanks. I'll get up earlier tomorrow. I thought we were off today."

"We always have to be ready at a minute's notice." She smiled at him as they rode off while he was taking another bite of the bread. "Do you like it?"

"Yeah, it's great."

"Good. I made it."

He was really glad he did then. "So what do we do with Orion once we rescue him?"

"If we can rescue him, we can take him somewhere that the creatures are a bit more hospitable. Which can be a challenge, but I'm sure we can find someplace to leave him."

"You know, if he found an elf he couldn't live without, that could solve our problem with him possibly wanting to steal Persephonice and take her back to her ship."

"Do you have anyone in mind?" Rina asked.

"Justina?"

"Princess Mirabella's new maid?" Rina shook her head. "It would be good if Orion went somewhere else and met someone. Not in either the Darkland elf or shadow elf kingdoms because of Persephonice and Eloria. He might not want to try and take Eloria back with him, but what if he did and forced Persephonice to return with him so Eloria would be allowed to come back to our world? So somewhere else."

"You know we are perfect for each other," Artur said.

"Hmm."

"I'm serious," Artur said.

"You have not even met all the shadow elf girls who live here."

Artur laughed. "There is no one who is exactly like you and that's what I love about you."

"I love you too."

Artur glanced at her and smiled.

She chuckled and shook her head. "We must wait."

"Until you are sure about me," Artur said with a sigh. He had not thought the girl he would fall in love with would have just ended a relationship with another guy.

"Until *we* are sure about *us*."

They rode in silence for several minutes.

"I am sure about you, us," Artur said.

"Okay, three weeks."

"Like your parents. We have already been together for a week."

She chuckled.

"So that means two more weeks," Artur said.

"If we can make it that long…" She turned her head to the south. "Do you hear Orion yelling? For help?"

"Aye. Let's go save a langolar and put him on a less

dangerous path, though as you say, our world can be rather hostile."

"That's why we need each other to help navigate the good and the bad. I never expected to meet my mate while rescuing a princess."

"I never expected to meet a warrior after my own heart."

EPILOGUE

Artur and Rina didn't make it two more weeks before they married. Rina had nothing to fear when it came to Artur's loyalty to her. Other girls didn't interest him, not when he had the greatest treasure of all. He hadn't meant to give Pascale a black eye either. It just happened. The guy shouldn't have spouted off to Artur about Rina's failings. Nobody was perfect, but Rina was as close as it came to that as far as Artur was concerned.

Even King Leogane and Queen Mirabella had gladly come to their wedding, which made it even more special and awed many of the shadow elves and the shadow elf king to no end. Justina was at Mirabella's beck and call if she needed her for anything, yet Mirabella wanted her to enjoy the festivities there too. The maid had become a whole different person now that she wasn't working for the tyrant Inari.

Now Rina's sister and her brother too were hoping to find a mate on their missions like Rina and their parents had done. Before that, they had thought their parents meeting and falling love had just been a fluke.

As to Orion, he and Rina had saved him from trolls and set

him on a different path in the land of the ice giants, cautioning him to move to somewhere safe when the giants were roaming about.

Artur and Rina no longer lived at the cabin, which was really just for temporary guests. They had built a home of their own on her parents' land with everyone's help. Being the king's champion had been a great thing, but having Rina in his life, was even greater.

Rina had thought accomplishing missions on her own was the only way to go, but now with Artur in her life, she loved their teamwork.

The next morning, she kissed Artur. "Were you planning on sleeping in?"

"Nay. Not if we have another mission."

"Dracolin came by the house and woke me. He said Orion is in need of rescuing again."

"Explorers explore, document their explorations, and some-times return home to share their stories, while others perish. I don't recall in our own history books that warriors were sent out to rescue an explorer who was always getting himself into trouble."

"Sometimes ships, men, and supplies were sent on rescue missions to save explorers. Remember, Orion is on his own without family or friends to come to his aid."

"You don't think Orion's cries for help are to get your atten-tion, do you?" Artur asked.

She smiled at him as she packed some food for them. "I should never had said in jest that I could be interested in a langolar. Besides, this one is way too needy and he's not a warrior."

Artur pulled her into his arms and kissed her. "Good. Are you ready to rescue him?"

"I am."

"And where should we leave him off this time?"

"How about somewhere more civilized and safe? The Black Hills kingdom or Castle Grande? Maybe they could benefit from his special gifts like we do with Persephonice?"

"Aye, we'll visit my old haunts and we'll be welcome. Oh, and Jeremka and Callie are wedding each other soon," Artur said.

"Then off to Castle Grande we go, after we rescue Orion once again," Rina said, climbing onto her horse, and Artur soon joined her.

"With a wedding after that and a feast to follow," Artur said.

"Now that's my kind of mission, especially when I have a champion to dance with. Well, not any king's champion, just you."

"Once you came into my life, I want to dance, when before I preferred to watch."

"It's a good thing too."

He laughed. He knew they were perfect for each other.

ACKNOWLEDGMENTS

Thanks to Darla Taylor and Donna Fournier for reading this right before Thanksgiving when everyone is thinking about family gatherings and gift giving for Christmas! I'm so thankful to you both!

AUTHOR BIO

USA Today bestselling and award-winning author **Terry Spear** has written over eighty paranormal romance novels, young adult, and medieval Highland historical romances. Her first werewolf romance, *Heart of the Wolf,* was named a 2008 *Publishers Weekly*'s Best Book of the Year, and her subsequent titles have garnered high praise and hit the *USA Today* bestseller list. A retired officer of the U.S. Army Reserves, Terry lives in Spring, Texas, where she is working on her next werewolf romance, shapeshifting jaguars, cougar shifters, vampires, hot Highlanders, and having fun with her young adult novels, helping with her grandchildren and raising two Havanese dogs. For more information, please visit www.terryspear.com, or follow her on Twitter, @TerrySpear. She is also on Facebook at https://www.facebook.com/TerrySpearParanormalRomantics. And on Wordpress at:

Terry Spear's Shifters

http://terryspear.wordpress.com/

And her Wilde & Woolley Bears, award-winning teddy bears, that have found homes all over the world: www.celticbears.com

ALSO BY TERRY SPEAR

Heart of the Cougar Series:

Cougar's Mate, Book 1

Call of the Cougar, Book 2

Taming the Wild Cougar, Book 3

Covert Cougar Christmas (Novella)

Double Cougar Trouble, Book 4

Cougar Undercover, Book 5

Cougar Magic, Book 6

Cougar Halloween Mischief (Novella)

Falling for the Cougar, Book 7

Catch the Cougar (A Halloween Novella)

Cougar Christmas Calamity Book 8

You Had Me at Cougar, Book 9

Saving the White Cougar, Book 10

Big Cat Magic, Book 11

Heart of the Bear Series

Loving the White Bear, Book 1

Claiming the White Bear, Book 2

The Highlanders Series:

Novella Prequels:

His Wild Highland #1, Vexing the Highlander #2

Winning the Highlander's Heart, The Accidental Highland Hero, Highland Rake, Taming the Wild Highlander, The Highlander, Her Highland Hero, The Viking's Highland Lass, My Highlander

Other historical romances: Lady Caroline & the Egotistical Earl, A Ghost of a Chance at Love

Heart of the Wolf Series: Heart of the Wolf, Destiny of the Wolf, To Tempt the Wolf, Legend of the White Wolf, Seduced by the Wolf, Wolf Fever, Heart of the Highland Wolf, Dreaming of the Wolf, A SEAL in Wolf's Clothing, A Howl for a Highlander, A Highland Werewolf Wedding, A SEAL Wolf Christmas, Silence of the Wolf, Hero of a Highland Wolf, A Highland Wolf Christmas, A SEAL Wolf Hunting; A Silver Wolf Christmas, A SEAL Wolf in Too Deep, Alpha Wolf Need Not Apply, Billionaire in Wolf's Clothing, Between a Rock and a Hard Place, SEAL Wolf Undercover, Dreaming of a White Wolf Christmas, Flight of the White Wolf, All's Fair in Love and Wolf, A Billionaire Wolf for Christmas, SEAL Wolf Surrender (2019), Silver Town Wolf: Home for the Holidays (2019), Wolff Brothers: You Had Me at Wolf, Night of the Billionaire Wolf, Joy to the Wolves (Red Wolf), The Wolf Wore Plaid, Jingle Bell Wolf, Best of Both Wolves, While the Wolf's Away, Christmas Wolf Surprise, Wolf Takes the Lead, Wolf on the Wild Side, Her Wolf for the Holidays (Highland Wolf, 2023)

SEAL Wolves: To Tempt the Wolf, A SEAL in Wolf's Clothing, A SEAL Wolf Christmas, A SEAL Wolf Hunting, A SEAL Wolf in Too Deep, SEAL Wolf Undercover, SEAL Wolf Surrender (2019)

Silver Bros Wolves: Destiny of the Wolf, Wolf Fever, Dreaming of the Wolf, Silence of the Wolf, A Silver Wolf Christmas, Alpha Wolf Need

Not Apply, Between a Rock and a Hard Place, All's Fair in Love and Wolf, Silver Town Wolf: Home for the Holidays

Wolff Brothers of Silver Town Wolff Brothers: You Had Me at Wolf, Jingle Bell Wolf, Wolf on the Wild Side

Arctic Wolves: Legend of the White Wolf, Dreaming of a White Wolf Christmas, Flight of the White Wolf, While the Wolf's Away

Billionaire Wolves: Billionaire in Wolf's Clothing, A Billionaire Wolf for Christmas, Night of the Billionaire Wolf, Wolf Takes the Lead

Highland Wolves: Heart of the Highland Wolf, A Howl for a Highlander, A Highland Werewolf Wedding, Hero of a Highland Wolf, A Highland Wolf Christmas, The Wolf Wore Plaid,

Red Wolf Series: Seduced by the Wolf, Joy to the Wolves (Red Wolf) Best of Both Wolves, Christmas Wolf Surprise,

Novellas: A United Shifter Force Christmas

Highland Wolves of Old: Wolf Pack (Book 1)

Heart of the Jaguar Series: Savage Hunger, Jaguar Fever, Jaguar Hunt, Jaguar Pride, A Very Jaguar Christmas, You Had Me at Jaguar

Novella: The Witch and the Jaguar

Dawn of the Jaguar

Romantic Suspense: Deadly Fortunes, In the Dead of the Night, Relative Danger, Bound by Danger

Vampire romances: Killing the Bloodlust, Deadly Liaisons, Huntress for Hire, Forbidden Love, Vampire Redemption, Primal Desire

Vampire Novellas: Vampiric Calling, The Siren's Lure, Seducing the Huntress

Other Romance: Exchanging Grooms, Marriage, Las Vegas Style

Science Fiction Romance: Galaxy Warrior

Teen/Young Adult/Fantasy Books

The World of Fae:

The Dark Fae, Book 1

The Deadly Fae, Book 2

The Winged Fae, Book 3

The Ancient Fae, Book 4

Dragon Fae, Book 5

Hawk Fae, Book 6

Phantom Fae, Book 7

Golden Fae, Book 8

Falcon Fae, Book 9

Woodland Fae, Book 10

Angel Fae, Book 11

The World of Elf:

The Shadow Elf

Darkland Elf

Warrior Elf

Blood Moon Series:

Kiss of the Vampire

The Vampire...In My Dreams

Demon Guardian Series:

The Trouble with Demons

Demon Trouble, Too

Demon Hunter

Non-Series for Now:

Ghostly Liaisons

The Beast Within

Courtly Masquerade

Deidre's Secret

The Magic of Inherian:

The Scepter of Salvation

The Mage of Monrovia

Emerald Isle of Mists